IRREVOCABLE

BOOK 7

THE BLOODLUST CHRONICLES

TARA VASSER

Copyright© Winter Musings LLC **2017**

978-0-9976475-4-9 - print
978-0-9976475-5-6 - ebook - epub
978-0-9976475-6-3 - ebook - mobi
978-0-9976475-7-0 - audiobook

Editing By: Beyond Def

Cover Art By: DuskTilDawn Designs

Photo Credit:

Royal Touch Photography

IRREVOCABLE

IRREVOCABLE IS A PREQUEL TO IRRESISTIBLE — BOOK ONE OF THE BLOODLUST CHRONICLES.
IT CAN BE READ AS A STANDALONE IF SO DESIRED.

INCLUDED IN THE BACK OF THIS WORK IS A SNEAK PEEK AT THE FIRST COUPLE CHAPTERS OF IRRESISTIBLE, BOOK 1 OF THE BLOODLUST CHRONICLES.

DEDICATION

To Tony – Thank you for being my real-life Viking,
complete with flowing tresses.

Acknowledgements

Special thanks go out to:

My beta readers for the wonderful insight you provide, you all are amazing!
The ladies at Beyond Def for putting up with my changes and indecision.
Dusk Til Dawn Designs – for both the cover and the advice – it is ALWAYS appreciated.
Wicked Leanore for the awesome formatting.
Royal Touch Photography for the spectacular photos.
Chase for sweating your ass off draped in fur for the photos.

As always – you – the reader! There are no words to express just how much you are appreciated.

IRREVOCABLE

Fallen in the heat of battle in King Harald's war, Endre lies in wait for the Valkyries to lead him to Valhalla. Instead of the beautiful warrior maidens of lore, Endre is visited by a mysterious stranger who grants him the gift of immortality.

Endre soon learns immortality comes with a thirst for blood which threatens to devour his remaining humanity. His only hope to retain any shred of his former self is to seek the destruction of the Vampire horde his mysterious benefactor unwillingly drafted him into.

The story of Endre's journey to immortality in this Prequel to Irresistible, book one of The Bloodlust Chronicles is rendered through a unique mixture of Viking and Vampire lore.

CHAPTER ONE

The force of his opponent's swing drove Endre a step backward, but he would not yield, nor would his blade. It was a rare occurrence to be locked in a duel with an adversary for any length of time on the battlefield. Hurtling through the mass of bodies and striking lethal blows to take out enemies was more his norm, which meant he was also subjected to the same brutal swarming and destruction of those he battled against, especially if he stayed in one place too long.

Endre threw every ounce of force and momentum of his body into a single shove to knock his opponent off balance. As the man stumbled, Endre took the opening, not allowing him to recover before his steel was buried deep in his belly. Coughing blood into his mangy beard, the man crumpled to the ground with a grunt of pain when Endre withdrew his sword from his body. There was no surprise in his eyes; they shone with unshed tears and resignation of his fate. Endre's opponent knew the odds of surviving a battle in King Fairhair's war were slim. Such was the way of war, and one had to be ever diligent if he expected to survive. Endre never expected to survive long, but that did not make him any less diligent.

Endre met another enemy's sword strike, dispatching the man with a well-placed thrust into the soft tissue above his collarbone before moving on to the next and the next. With his double-edged blade in one hand and his shield deflecting the attacks of his enemies, he was a killing machine— heartless and as cold as the snow-frosted ground they fought upon. It was how he and his fellow men-at-arms stayed alive, by turning their hearts to ice on the battlefield. There was no time to register and weigh the emotions that came with the taking of a life in the heat of battle. There were always more men waiting behind the one he felled to take their turn attempting to spill his blood and send him to Valhalla.

A shout behind him drew his attention, and Endre quickly whirled around to block a blow with his shield. The gods were after him today. He was not ready to take his place in the Hall of Heroes quite yet, though. He struck out at the man before him like a berserker, ending his life before he knew what had hit him. Endre's frenzied energy earned him the collapse of two more of his enemies, taking the head off the last one before it happened.

Searing pain ripped through Endre's midsection, a dire reminder of his mortality delivered by the blade of an enemy. He bellowed at the agony of the intrusion. Wet warmth spread across the skin of his belly, a stark contrast to the cold air around him. Endre knew without looking it was blood—his blood—but he looked anyway. Pressing his hand over where a sword had impaled him only moments ago, Endre brought his crimson-stained fingers into his line of sight. He could see nothing else. Could focus on nothing else. He'd seen plenty of blood on the battlefield, but never from his own fatal wound. I am going to die. The realization should have shocked him, but he'd prepared himself for this eventuality the moment he first stepped foot onto this field of thick mud.

Endre's focus moved from his fingers to the man who had taken his world from him. To the man he would take into death alongside him. Without thought or remorse, the arm that still grasped his sword tightly swung of its own accord, severing his enemy's head from his body. Endre watched the head roll away, an expression of almost comical surprise with eyes and mouth open wide, frozen on the flesh, and he envied the man.

His death was quick and painless. Endre's would not be so.

Endre collapsed to his knees under the weight of his own pain, splashing mud and blood and other substances he did not even want to consider. His stomach rebelled against the stench of death and decay, threatening to add its contents to the mire in which he knelt. The agony radiating from his guts was excruciating in this position, and he could not hold it for long. He stared once more at the dark stains on his hands from his lifeblood. It was once his favorite color—that deep red which reminded him of life and warmth—but outside his body it served only as a reminder death was coming for him.

The world started to tilt, and Endre could not stop himself from falling to his back to face the sky. It was a beautiful day. He could not have picked a more vibrant day to die. The sun blazed brightly overhead in the cloudless expanse, reflecting off the dense blanket of snow covering the ground, making it impossible to see white snow, as it was white no longer. The mud and blood mixed together with the shit and piss of the dead and dying, turning it into a putrid color that had no name.

The absence of battle sounds nearby broke Endre's eye contact with the sun, an eternal staring contest he could never hope to win. All around him the stench of defeat permeated his pores, the sounds of steel clanging against steel were far off in the distance, but the noise of suffering was all around him—a dismal chorus of moans and muffled cries Endre had unwillingly joined. He focused on the sounds of the battle still raging between men to block out the one between man and death he was now embroiled in, but there was no use. Soon, those sounds dimmed, replaced by the rushing waves of his blood in his ears that reminded him of the rhythmic beat of sea against shore. It calmed him for a time, until even that dissipated in favor of a violent ringing only he could hear—his death knell. Endre closed his eyes, death reaching for him down to his bones, and he embraced it with what was left of his being. There was nothing left to do now but wait.

Behind his eyelids, he could pretend he would still return home a celebrated hero. The allure of Valhalla was tempting, but the promise of the warmth of his wife's embrace was even more so. Ingrid. It had been months since he'd left their home, destined for battle, but not a single day went by when he did not think of her. Most nights he dreamt of her green eyes and the ecstasy they sparkled with when he was buried deep inside her. Many nights they'd attempted to conceive a son, but she was still without child when he'd ventured away. Endre had hoped they could continue the pursuit when he returned, but now he would leave this world, and his bloodline with him. *I love you, Ingrid, my wife,* Endre whispered to her memory in his mind.

CHAPTER TWO

A sound pierced the dark blanket of unconsciousness in which Endre was enveloped. His eyes shuttered, he could not place the source of it. It sounded again, and with an effort possessed only by the mighty Thor, Endre pried his eyes open. The brightness around him after the dark he had embraced burned his eyes, making him squint. The call came again, and this time he saw dark wings, black as pitch, circling above him. His eyes moved lazily, following the flight pattern. Was this a crow, come to feast on his flesh before he even left it, or a raven sending a message from Odin himself? He cursed his inability to identify the language it spoke.

"Hel or Valhalla?" Endre's raspy whisper sounded foreign in his ears.

"Neither, at least at the moment," a rough voice answered.

Endre blinked up at the scavenger hovering over him, struggling to decipher the bird's answer. Movement to his right caught his attention. A man, too clean and unmarred to be on a battlefield, crouched beside him, and Endre realized it must have been this man who had answered his uttered question. Endre watched with macabre fascination as the man revealed sharp fangs and tore into the flesh of his own arm. He had seen enemies file their teeth to appear more fearsome, but he had never seen them cannibalize their own flesh. Blood oozed between the sharp points, and Endre could not bring himself to turn away. In the blink of an eye, the man brought his bloodstained wrist to Endre's mouth, dripping his blood into it. He did not even get the chance to fight before his mouth was filled. His arms were leaden and he could not move them to push the man away. Instead, he choked on the warm liquid, nausea churning in his stomach, but swallowed it down to continue taking air into his lungs. Endre lost track of how many times he swallowed.

"Enough," the man whispered to him, pulling his hand away.

He rose to his feet, towering over Endre's prone body, staring. Waiting. Strange sensations coursed through his body within moments. His limbs no longer felt heavy, but they warmed like he'd just had a deep flagon of the finest ale. The warmth gave way to an itching sensation at the site of his fatal wound, and Endre felt the skin stretch.

He lifted his hand to touch the wound, looking up in awe at the man who still hovered above him. He was smiling now, but with his vision cleared, Endre could see hollow darkness in those eyes that did not belong in the world of mortals. Evil lurked in those depths, the likes of which Endre had never seen before. The man offered Endre his hand. Endre grasped it tightly and was pulled to his feet as if it were no effort at all. Now that he was standing, he could once again see his injury. He gaped in shock and surprise as the gruesome gash pulled together and sealed his insides off from the world once again. Was he in the presence of one of the gods? Endre did not recognize his likeness.

"Very good!" the god exclaimed with a chuckle, exuding warmth that did not match the coldness in his eyes. "You will do nicely."

The god surveyed Endre, and Endre could only imagine what it was he saw that pleased him so. Endre was covered in the same muck as the bodies of the dead and dying surrounding him on the battlefield; he wondered what it was that made him worthy of saving. When his eyes met with his savior again, he found dead eyes boring into his, reaching into the very depths of his being as if to snatch back the life he had just returned to Endre. A smile filled with cruelty and malice pulled up the corner of the god's lips and with movement faster than Endre thought possible, the god's hands rested on either side of Endre's head. One last glimpse into his eyes, and Endre realized it was not a god that had saved him, but a demon that prolonged his death sentence. The demon twisted his hands, and the familiar sound of snapping bone reached Endre's ears a second before he registered it was his own broken neck that killed him.

CHAPTER THREE

Endre groaned at the throbbing which had taken up residence in his head. It pounded so fiercely, he could pay attention to nothing else around him.

"One of the new recruits is waking," a gravelly voice said from somewhere nearby.

"Feed him, and then get him over to The Master," a second, higher, voice answered.

A cold hand slapped at his cheek. Endre's eyes flew open at the sudden assault, his body jerking away from a second anticipated hit. He nearly screamed as he registered burning pain radiating throughout the entirety of his body, down to the marrow of his bones.

"Drink," Gravelly Voice ordered, holding up a flagon to Endre's lips.

The skin on Endre's lips cracked as he opened to take in whatever nourishment he was being provided; his mouth felt dry as sand. Thick, warm liquid flooded his mouth, the metallic tang unmistakable. Blood. He lurched away from the vessel, spilling the vile substance down his front and spitting what coated his mouth to the ground beside him. A heavy hand knocked him upside the head, bringing his attention back to the raspy-voiced man.

"Do not waste it, you idiot!" The man shook his head and offered the flagon once more, this time giving Endre the choice to take it or not. "You need it, trust me."

Trust him? Endre had no idea who this man was, where they were, or what in Hel was going on. He tried to come up with the last memory he could recall—settling on the image of the demon breaking his neck and taking away the life he'd bestowed on him only moments prior. Was this a game demons played? Heal the mortally wounded, only to take the lives with their own hands instead?

"Listen," the man said, and Endre could see the remnants of compassion in his eyes beneath the darkened pupils, "the blood is part of the process. If you do not take the blood, you do not live. You want to live?"

Endre didn't know how to answer honestly. If he lived, would he be at the mercy of the demon who slew him? He opened his mouth to ask, but it was so dry no sound came forth. The man raised the flagon of blood again as he raised his eyebrows. It was then Endre realized he did not have a choice.

He nodded to the other man, and the flagon was pressed into his hand. It shook as he brought the rim to his lips, trying to hold off the nausea that rolled through him when he felt the blood flood his mouth, flowing into every crevice. By the time he took the first swallow, his sickness was gone, replaced by a thirst so great he thought he may never quench it. He quickly drained the flagon and held it out to the man, who still watched him closely.

"Is there more?" Endre inquired, his throat burning with the need to consume more.

The man clapped him on the shoulder and smiled. "You will get plenty more after you meet with The Master. Welcome, brother, you are one of us now. I am Gunnar."

"Endre," Endre answered automatically.

Gunnar took the flagon from Endre's hand and held out his open one as an offer to help Endre stand. Endre was struck with how easily Gunnar pulled him to his feet, just like the man from the battlefield.

"Are you a demon?" Endre asked, not realizing he had spoken the words aloud until he saw the surprised look on Gunnar's face.

"Same as you," Gunnar responded cryptically, guiding him toward the flap in the tent that led them outdoors.

It was the dead of night outside; no sounds but the predators of the night could be heard. The night sky was clear, the stars providing the only illumination. It was the time when the moon was dark, but Endre could see as if it were daylight. It was astonishing to know he would never again be plagued by the darkness that came with night. Gunnar led him to one of the other tents in solemn silence, giving Endre an uneasy sense of foreboding. He still had not the faintest idea what was happening, and he longed for the weight of his sword in his hand if for nothing more than the comfort of the ability to defend himself against an unknown foe.

Gunnar stopped outside one of the tents and held the flap open, ushering Endre inside before him. Endre eyed him warily, having been a warrior long enough to be hesitant to turn his back to a yet unproven friend. Gunnar made an impatient motion to encourage Endre to step over the threshold. Endre hesitated for only a moment before taking a stride into the tent.

"Master," Gunnar spoke with the reverence Endre only reserved for the gods and his wife.

A figure cloaked in fur stood with his back to them, a horrid squelching emanating from him. A rapidly slowing heartbeat rang loudly in Endre's ears. Where is the device producing such an eerie noise hidden? The man before them lifted his head, his gaze reaching the ceiling, and let out a contented sigh. The man dropped something with a heavy thud at his feet before he turned to face them. Endre's eyes were drawn to that discarded item, only to see a very feminine arm lying still on the ground, the rest of her body shielded from his view by the man's furs.

"You have killed hundreds of men in battle, and yet you are squeamish at the sight of a single body. I do not understand it," the man said, drawing Endre's attention away from the woman's lifeless arm.

Endre no longer heard the heartbeat which had unnerved him when he entered the tent. There were only three now, beating strong and steady, the rhythmic sound filling his body's entire capacity of audition. That fourth heartbeat, the one that labored to continue when he'd stepped over the threshold, had belonged to the woman and had now silenced.

Endre's gaze went to the man who had committed the atrocity, and his rage at having been unable to prevent the murder was near to boiling over. Endre stared at the man, his anger momentarily overridden by his shock before fury took its place again.

"You!" he shouted, rushing toward the man who had broken his neck on the battlefield.

CHAPTER FOUR

The man chuckled and stepped to the side, but
Endre moved with him. Gunnar, however, was
there to restrain him in less than the time required
to take a breath. Endre had moved faster than he
had ever been able to before, and these men moved
the same. He stared down at his hands, as if seeing
them for the first time. Indeed, they appeared the
same as they had in life, but now there was
something different beneath the callused skin.
More strength. More speed. Less human.

"What manner of demon are you?" Endre
bellowed, struggling against the steel grip of
Gunnar's arms.

The man smiled at him, the same cold, devious
smile he'd presented Endre with before he'd
broken his neck.

"I am your Master. And you, my minion, are
now a part of my Vampire horde," the one they
called Master told him.

Endre stumbled backward a step, pushing
Gunnar with him in his shock. He was a Vampire?

A Vampire—a demon that lived a second life beyond death, feeding off the lives of innocents. His gaze went to the woman lying on the floor, drained of blood. Endre was the same kind of evil now, transformed by the blood Master had pooled into his mouth. Endre's head spun with the knowledge that this was his fate now, to have to murder in order to survive. He was no stranger to taking lives, but there was a fundamental difference between taking the life of a warrior who understood the risk to life and limb on the battlefield and stealing a life to prolong his own.

"I have something for you, a welcome gift," The Master said, that cruel smile breaking across his face again.

The flap to the tent flipped open and another man—Vampire, Endre corrected himself—came in, dragging a bound woman. The woman looked around the tent in panic, horror evident in her features. Her eyes landed on the woman The Master had devoured, her body fully visible now that he'd moved to circle around Endre. The woman shrieked a blood-curdling scream, and The Master laughed maniacally, dragging her close by the rope binding despite her struggle. With that sick grin still in place, he wrapped a hand around her throat and lifted her to balance on just her toes, cutting off her scream.

"Pathetic, are they not?" he said, examining the woman with a mixture of wonder and disgust. Her eyes were wide and fearful, her complexion reddening with the lack of breath. "You are no longer one of them. You are no longer livestock," he said, dropping his hand from the woman's neck. She fell to the ground, gasping and coughing. "You proved yourself on the battlefield. You cut through your enemies like a butcher cleaving apart a carcass. I enjoyed watching you. I waited on the outskirts of many battles to see you fall so I could bring you into the fold. Your brutality will be an asset here. I am curious to see what you do with this one. She is yours to do with as you wish. Anything you wish," he offered, an impossibly dark gleam in his eyes.

Endre could not mistake The Master's unspoken meaning behind his words. He expected Endre to rape and kill the woman. And The Master expected to watch. Gunnar's arms dropped from around him, and Endre felt him take a step back. He did not look to confirm, his eyes still riveted on The Master.

"No," Endre whispered, "I may be a monster in form, but I will not become one by action."

"No?" The Master asked, his tone menacing. "I give you the gift of immortality and that gift is irrevocable. I brought you back from the clutches

~ 18 ~

of death itself and you dare throw it back in my face? I made you. I own you. You will obey my commands!" he roared with rage.

"I will not harm an innocent woman!" Endre yelled in response.

The Master reached to the ground and yanked the woman to her feet again. She whimpered but otherwise made no other noise. He held her with her back pressed to his front, his fingers holding her chin so she could not look away from Endre.

"Innocent? None of them are innocents. They have all lied, cheated, stolen, or fornicated. Taste her blood and you will see the innocence you protect. Go on, taste her," The Master encouraged.

Endre remained rooted in place, his hands curled into fists at his sides. It was likely he would die a second time at The Master's hands if he did not do as he was bid. He was prepared for that. He may no longer hold a seat in Valhalla, but he would not do something to secure one in Hel.

The Master produced a blade from beneath his cloak, and before Endre could intervene, he made a slice along the column of the woman's throat, his hand muffling the woman's screams. The cut drew blood but was not deep enough to kill.

"You can spare her pain if your soft heart desires," The Master said.

Endre's eyes locked on the rivulet of blood dripping down the woman's throat. A burning sensation spread through Endre as he watched the droplets of blood trickle slowly down her skin. The longer he watched, the more intense it was, as though the very marrow of his bones was on fire.

"You can make her want you," The Master continued, "but once you get a taste, you may no longer care."

Tears flowed down her face, faster than the blood dripping from her neck, as if in a race. Endre glanced at her tears for but a moment before his attention was once again rapt on the red lines reaching her collarbone. Such a beautiful shade of red. It was his favorite once, and on her, dripping from her, he considered it his favorite once again. The Master shoved her toward Endre and he caught her in his arms as she collided with him. Her tear-streaked face was turned up to him, her eyes pleading for mercy. But Endre no longer saw her eyes. Only the blood. Up close, the smell of those tiny droplets was potent and overwhelmed his senses. Up close, he could see the sheen of the blood and watched it continue to well from the shallow cut. Up close, he felt his resolve waver. His entire being burned to taste her on his tongue, to drink those droplets and feel them sliding down his throat. It was all he could think about now, his mind singularly focused on what flowed through her veins.

"Taste," The Master ordered with an air of impatience.

Endre no longer had the will to refuse. He leaned toward her, inhaling the scent of his new brand of sustenance. Then he ran his tongue along the cut, collecting the streams before they could be wasted. When he swallowed, he felt the burning ebb slightly. It was a tease. He needed more. Sharp pain erupted from his mouth as bone pushed through skin, revealing a set of fangs identical to The Master's. Endre ran his tongue along the sharp points, admiring their ferocity. These were his new weapons, marking him as one of the Vampires. He could no longer deny what he was, and in that moment he no longer wanted to.

Locking his arms around the woman, Endre once again lowered his mouth to her neck. Running his fangs along her skin, he tested their sharpness, pleased to see the marks they left. She let out a cry, begging him to spare her. He did not hear the words; he heard only her heart as it beat in time to the pulsing of the vessel in her neck. Only skin separated him from the blood he needed, and Endre intended to take it. With a vicious growl, he plunged his fangs into her skin and tore it away to get to what he wanted. What he needed. He barely took notice of the scream that would have deafened a mere man. His sole focus was on the blood that now flowed from her into his mouth, quenching the fire within him as he greedily drew it from her.

Swallow after swallow, Endre drew the woman's life into his own body. Her screams dissipated and her limbs grew slack. The sound of her heartbeat slowed in his ears with each draft he pulled. Soon, her heart ceased to beat altogether. When he could not pull another drop from her, he dropped her limp body to the ground. Closing his eyes, Endre merely felt the blood rejuvenating his body, strengthening it beyond what it was ever capable of before. The pain in his bones disappeared and his veins felt tight with the onslaught of fresh life pumping through them. Her blood completed his transformation to one of the deadliest of creatures with senses to rival other predators roaming nearby.

Heartbeats of the small animals taking refuge in the surrounding woods echoed in Endre's head, louder than they ought to be. Smoke from fires land-miles away filled his nostrils, carrying with it the scent of melting fat dripping into the flames. Small currents of air swirled over his skin with each movement of the other Vampires in the tent, providing a mental map of the location of each body.

The Master clapped his hands, breaking into Endre's trance. "That was simply magnificent," he chuckled with glee. "I knew my decision to spare you would not be in vain."

The red haze clouding his mind slowly dissipated, and Endre opened his eyes to find The Master grinning that sinister smile at him. Gunnar stood by with a stoic expression, but Endre could barely remember what had transpired before he had closed them. His gaze was drawn to the body at his feet and he froze. His vision was sharper than it had ever been. He could see everything about the woman—the individual fibers of the dress she wore, the strands of gray hair hiding amongst the brown, the tiny crevices in the skin around her mouth that showed how often she had laughed before he'd taken that away from her. Her life had been snuffed out by his hands, his fangs. He had taken her life and solidified his place among the monsters; there was no reversing it.

"You are one of us now," The Master whispered in front of him. Endre tore his gaze from the woman he'd murdered and met The Master's. "Now go, you will need rest to complete the transition. Tomorrow night we will discuss strategy."

The Master dismissed him with a wave of his hand, and Gunnar took Endre's arm, guiding him through the exit of the tent.

"I am a monster," Endre whispered to his companion.

"We all are," Gunnar agreed, his gaze on the glow of the impending sunrise at the horizon.

CHAPTER FIVE

Gunnar brought Endre to another tent and pointed at a corner on the ground.

"We sleep here until sunset," Gunnar stated, then took his place on the packed earth.

Endre lay on the hard, cold earth, trying to remember what it felt like to sleep on something as simple as a pallet.

"You will get used to it," Gunnar reassured him, as if reading his thoughts.

Endre merely grunted his assent before lacing his fingers behind his head and staring into the roof of the tent, imagining he could see the oranges and pinks of the sunrise bleeding through it. Perhaps he could with this transformed eyesight of his. He tried to keep the image of the woman from his mind, but it haunted him. He tried to collect the snippets of memory he had lost after the first taste of her blood, coming up with fragmented frames drowned in red. He had been a beast possessed, his will taken from him by the monster he had become.

He closed his eyes, trying to block out the images and found, to his surprise, exhaustion under the surface. Soon, sleep took him under and folded him in her serene blanket. It was a relief from the inner turmoil he was certain would eat him alive from the inside.

A quiet humming filled Endre's head, the sound sweet and melodic. His gaze went to the potato he peeled in his hand. His hands were small and delicate but worked with a practiced pace. The blade skimmed across the surface of the vegetable, taking just enough of the skin without wasting too much of the meat. He watched in fascination as he made quick work of one potato, and then another. He could not remember having peeled a potato since he was a child, and he wondered how he had become so adept at it.

A crash sounded in the distance, making him jump. A string of low curses came from his mouth in a voice not his own. The voice had a familiarity about it he could not quite place, but he didn't have time to contemplate it further when his gaze was drawn down to the blood that welled from a cut on those soft hands. He must have cut himself when he had been startled. Another curse dropped from his lips in that sweet voice and Endre wondered why he should dream himself a woman. He went to a basin of water and cleaned the cut, watching the red swirl and mix with the crystal-clear water, staining it a faint pink.

"Olav?" his dream voice asked. He walked to a door, opening it to reveal bright sunlight and warm air.

Endre stuck his head out the door and looked back and forth for the source of the disturbance. Seeing nothing, he pulled the door closed and turned around. Letting out a yelp of surprise when a figure stood in his path, his hand flew over his heart as if to stop it from leaping out of his body.

"Goodness," he whispered, and then, "Who are you?" to the menacing figure.

The figure merely smiled from the shadows, and Endre felt a pang of fear. This man was there to hurt him; he could see it in his eyes.

"Stay away from me!" Endre's dream voice shouted, backing away from the man.

The man lunged forward, and on reflex, Endre stabbed the knife he still held in his hand into the man's chest. The man gave out a cry of surprise and looked down at the protruding blade before collapsing to the floor as Endre screamed a hysterical feminine wail.

Endre sat up in his corner of the tent with a gasp, the sound of screaming from his dream still ringing in his ears. He'd had plenty of nightmares where he would see the men he had killed in battle, but nothing quite like that.

"It was a blood memory," Gunnar's voice came from a few feet away.

Endre looked to where the other Vampire lay on the ground on his side, staring at him.

"A what?" Endre asked.

"If I had to wager, I would say you just had a dream where you were not yourself," Gunnar guessed quite correctly.

Endre shook his head to try to clear the fog of sleep from it. "I think I was a woman," he answered.

Gunnar nodded in a knowing fashion. "You were seeing a memory of hers," Gunnar told him.

"Whose?" Endre asked, still not quite awake enough to follow the conversation clearly.

"The woman from the tent, the one you drank from," he said, nodding his head in the direction of the tent where The Master was located. "You will get them from time to time. They are memories the blood keeps. They show you a person's past where they have either spilled their blood or another's."

"Will I see them every time I … drink?" Endre asked uneasily.

Gunnar shook his head. "No, after a while your mind will learn how to move past them altogether, unless it is a particularly strong memory. Sometimes those come unbidden. You are sure as the daylight to have one of The Master's the next time you close your eyes. His are the most grisly."

That did not give Endre much comfort. The last thing he wanted was to see inside The Master's mind.

"How long?" Endre asked, thinking about the day when his mind would be strong enough to sweep the memories of others aside.

"Until?" Gunnar asked, his eyebrows raised.

"I do not see them anymore?" Endre completed his thought.

"Seems to be different for each of us. Some it takes only a few weeks, others have gone months experiencing one every night," Gunnar told him with a shrug.

"How long have you been a Vampire?" Endre asked, an itching sense of curiosity baiting him to ask the question.

"Two months. Not long," Gunnar said, his expression forlorn.

"Do you still have the nightmares?" Endre asked.

"I do," Gunnar admitted sourly.

"What are we doing here?" Endre asked him while idly wondering how far he would get if he tried to run.

"It would be best if I let The Master tell you about his grand plans," Gunnar said, repositioning on the cold ground. "Best to get some rest, too. There are still a few hours of daylight left, then you will find out what this is all about."

Gunnar closed his eyes again, their conversation at an end. Endre lay back down on the cold ground and closed his eyes. He prayed to the gods that had abandoned him to the keeping of a demon to banish any more of these blood memories from his dreams.

CHAPTER SIX

The sun sank toward the western horizon, heralding the oncoming night. Endre was awakened by the camp's stirring inhabitants as soon as twilight fell. Tent flaps swishing with the movement of soldiers walking past them and the footfalls of nearly silent wraiths sounded loudly in Endre's ears. For a moment, it was hard for him to place all the sounds; they were things he ought not to be able to hear. He sat in his spot on the cold ground, eyes closed, tilting his head to take in each noise and marvel at the clarity.

"You can damn near hear a mouse pissing in the ground with this cursed hearing," Gunnar grumbled next to Endre, diverting Endre's attention from the world outside their tent.

Endre opened his eyes to find his new comrade in arms staring at him with a troubled expression.

"What is it?" Endre asked after a few moments of silence stretched between them.

"The Master has called for you," Gunnar stated, the frown on his face deepening further.

"He said as much when I spoke with him last night," Endre said slowly, not entirely understanding where the issue lay.

"He does not typically attend to the new recruits after the initial feeding. He usually hands them over to those of us who have been here longest for us to teach his laws and the operations of the horde and camp logistics," Gunnar commented, stroking his chin thoughtfully.

"Should I be concerned?" Endre asked.

"All I am saying is you should be careful. Watch your back," Gunnar replied in a whisper barely above silence. A whisper anyone listening, uninvited, to their conversation would not be able to hear.

Endre nodded, not trusting himself with words. He rose to his feet and exited the tent, unsure which direction The Master's tent was located. He stood for a moment, taking in the sounds and honing in on the cadence and voice he knew belonged to the leader of this horde. Endre's strides were lithe and quick as he glided over the frosted ground toward the tent. He found once he arrived he did not require the announcement of the guard; The Master spoke to him through the barrier of the tent.

"You may enter," The Master announced, and the guard pulled back the flap for Endre to enter.

Endre strode inside, steeling himself for the sight of corpses littering the ground, but he was surprised when he found none. After surveying the contents of the tent, he faced The Master. Endre stood with his feet affixed to the earth at the width of his shoulders, his hands clasped behind his back, his dagger in close proximity should he be attacked.

"Master," Endre addressed him with a slight bow of his head. He had no idea what The Master had in store for him, but he was not dense enough to provoke his wrath with disrespect before he had a chance to assess the situation.

The Master smiled at him knowingly before turning his back to take a few strides to an ornately carved chair placed in the center of the room.

"A proper warrior," The Master mused, looking Endre over while he brushed his fingers along his lips as if deep in thought. "Your performances continue to impress me, Endre. First, on the battlefield, then yesterday, here, in this very tent, and today with your acceptance of your new lot. This tells me you are not only strong in body but also strong in mind. Many of those I have welcomed into this horde only possess the first strength. Some of them are not even great warriors, but they will do. It is no matter they are poorly trained in the arts of war, a Vampire warrior, even the worst one, can still decimate a human army. So, you see, I have no shortage of bodies to choose from. What I have been missing from this campaign is the keen intellect I see within you. I have a need for one who is well versed in strategy. A leader. That is why you are here, Endre. That is why I chose you," The Master said, his eyes refocusing on Endre.

"Perhaps if I knew more …" Endre started carefully, not wishing to enrage The Master. He was not usually so docile, but knowing that, in an instant, this second chance could be taken from him with but a whispered order from The Master, he was inclined to play his part.

"A soldier does not question the why of his orders," The Master warned, his glare boring into the very heart of Endre.

Endre refused to turn away. He understood The Master's game. He'd stated he wanted a leader, not another soldier. A leader does not follow blindly. A leader, Endre had been taught, always asked why. When Endre did not back down from their stalemate, The Master's face broke out into the eerie smile that would make a lesser man's skin crawl.

"Come, I will show you where you will train Vampires to become true warriors," The Master said, rising from his chair. "We will get to the why in due time."

Endre followed The Master from the tent out into the night. They wove between several other tents, where soldiers stopped mid-stride to bow to their Master and new commander. The feeling of being bowed to along with The Master unnerved Endre—he did not want to believe he was of the same ilk—but The Master had shown him a side of himself he had not known lurked inside him. The Master halted at the edge of the camp facing an expanse of browned grass that was matted from the trample of footsteps, the snow now having been ground into nothingness.

"Here is where you will instruct the Vampires to fight as you fight. You have more skill on the battlefield than any of my others have exhibited. As Vampires, we are nearly unstoppable to humans, but we will need to be more honed if we are to win the war to come," The Master said, gesturing to the clearing.

Endre assessed the area, calculating how many men he could train in the small space to ensure enough room to practice footwork without getting in the way of each other. He figured he could accommodate a hundred at the most.

"How many men?" Endre asked, still staring into the grass.

"Not men, Commander. Vampires. Men are of no consequence. Men are our food," The Master corrected, and Endre could hear the smile in his words.

"How many Vampires?" Endre revised.

"Your addition makes eighty-seven," The Master told him. Endre could see The Master studying him from the periphery of his vision. Endre imagined his expression must have spoken his thoughts aloud when The Master let out a hearty laugh. "You wonder why so few? Hmm?"

Endre nodded, unnerved The Master could read him so easily, and he wondered—not for the first time—what powers his demon-kind possessed he had yet to discover.

"We can easily overpower any human opposition, even numbered in the thousands. You have seen only a taste of what you can do as a Vampire. Our speed, our strength, and our senses are superb," The Master said, a note of pride in his voice. "But we are not concerned about humans," The Master continued.

"If not humans, who?" Endre asked as he turned to face The Master.

"What, is the correct question, Commander," The Master said with a grin. "Vampires. And those who hunt Vampires."

"How many do our opposition number?" Endre asked, folding his arms across his chest as he turned his body to face The Master.

"The opposing Vampire numbers are not as significant as our own. They have not organized. To my knowledge, they do not know we have organized, and we must act quickly if we are to catch them unawares. You will begin training them tomorrow night. Gunnar will familiarize you with the workings of the camp tonight," The Master said, gesturing for them to return their walk the way they had come.

"And what of those who hunt Vampires?" Endre inquired.

"They are merely humans who have an awareness of our kind and need to be eradicated," The Master said, waving his hand in the air as if shooing an insect away.

They walked through the camp in silence, Endre mulling over the task ahead of him and his unanswered questions. When they reached The Master's tent, Gunnar was already waiting for them.

"I will expect nightly reports," The Master ordered before disappearing into his tent.

Endre looked to Gunnar, who gestured they move away from the tent.

CHAPTER SEVEN

"Commander," Gunnar said, leading Endre through the maze of tents. "This is where new recruits are brought after The Master delivers them from the battlefields." He gestured to a tent Endre vaguely remembered from his initial arrival at the camp.

They moved on from the tent, and Endre noted there was no one in it. Gunnar led them to the edge of the camp, on the side opposite the training field The Master showed him earlier, and opened his arms, calling Endre's attention to the woods. For the first time, Endre noticed their camp was situated in a clearing encompassed by a circle of trees.

"Sentries guard the camp all around the perimeter," Gunnar stated, gesturing to about ten men Endre could pick out if he looked hard enough. "We have not seen any humans venture this way for about a week. There have been rumors floating around the nearby villages that this part of the woods is haunted. Stories about people wandering off and never coming back."

"Were they eaten?" Endre asked, thinking about the unsuspecting humans who'd wandered right into the midst of a Vampire army.

"Aye," Gunnar acknowledged with a nod. "Though, only the blood. We do not eat the flesh."

"What happens to the bodies?" Endre asked, his morbid curiosity getting the better of him.

"We bury them beneath the trees," Gunnar told him with a shrug. "Deep enough the wolves do not dig them back up. Not that we have seen any wolves around these parts since we set up camp. They seem to be able to sense us and stay out of our way. I suppose that is the way nature works, though, the smaller predator leaving the larger one be."

Endre nodded thoughtfully before turning his attention back to the sentries. "What happens during daylight?"

"The sentries, you mean?" Gunnar said.

"I mean the whole camp," Endre clarified, genuinely curious. He had only been a Vampire for a short time, and he did not really understand all it entailed. He only knew the legends he had heard about his new brethren and how they could not withstand the light of the sun. It was said such creatures of darkness could not be out in the open when there was sunlight or they would burn up.

"The men are ordered to sleep," Gunnar started, and Endre noted he still referred to them as "men," the same mistake Endre had made when he had addressed The Master. "We keep a few men in rotation on the perimeter to ensure we do not have any surprise visitors during the day, though with it being winter, those hours are few. The sentries would detect the incoming hostiles only a few moments before the camp would be roused. The scent of a human is enough to wake sleeping Vampires."

"They do not burn up? Out in the sun?" Endre asked, thoroughly surprised.

"No, as long as they stay in the shadows of the trees when the sun is out, they are not bothered by it. The legends were wrong about us, Commander, we do not turn to ash in the sunlight," Gunnar informed.

"What else were the legends wrong about, Gunnar?" Endre wondered aloud.

"We still look like men, for one," Gunnar stated, looking down at his own hands.

"Nor do we live in graves," Endre stated, needing to catalog this new life. "But there seems to be truth in the idea we can enter into the dreams of others." Endre thought about the blood memory and what Gunnar had told him. It seemed it was only a matter of time before Endre saw a bit of The Master's past from his blood.

"Aye," Gunnar whispered, and Endre could see the ghosts of the blood memories he had seen cloud his eyes. "I have also never seen Vampires change form, but I am still young, as measured by The Master's standards," Gunnar continued, alluding to the lore which stated a Vampire could alter appearance and crush their victims with their bodies.

Endre supposed all lore was steeped in truth. He had not seen any Vampires shapeshift, either—not in the way the legends stated—but he knew they were stronger; he would easily be able to crush a human with nothing but his bare hands. Endre shook his head to clear the sickening images of crushing humans into a pulpy mess and continued with his onslaught of questions for Gunnar.

"What about other Vampires? Not from the horde?" Endre asked, thinking about what The Master had told him about who their real enemy was.

"We have not seen any come within a few land-miles of the camp where the sentries are stationed," Gunnar replied.

"How would they be addressed?" Endre asked, wanting to ensure there was a protocol in place if one were to happen close enough to the camp to detect their numbers.

"They would be taken prisoner and brought to The Master, I would imagine," Gunnar said.

If other Vampires were the enemy, it did not make sense to have them captured with the off-chance they could escape and send warning to an army The Master seemed to be preparing for.

"I will address the need to take more drastic measure with The Master," Endre stated, thinking perhaps it would be in their best interest to terminate any foreign Vampires on site, rather than attempt to capture one.

Gunnar nodded his assent and looked to Endre for the next in the line of questions. Endre recognized Gunnar for the intelligent man he was and wondered where he had come from. But those were questions for another time.

"How is the horde fed?" Endre asked, dreading the answer to the question. Not only did the talk of feeding stoke a great burning in his throat, but he was also loath to learn how an army of eighty-seven Vampires maintained a food supply without decimating the local populations.

The more Endre thought about it, the more sense it made. If one were thinking in terms of the laws of nature and predators, it was wholly unnatural to have a host of Vampires. In nature, the food chain was such that predators numbered far fewer than prey. This amassing of Vampires was not sustainable. Their food supply would soon run out if they slaughtered all the humans around them. They would have to continue to move to eat, just as humans had done to follow herds of animals they fed off of.

"We have a group of men that hunts daily," Gunnar said, breaking into Endre's thoughts. There it was again, the word that no longer encompassed them—men.

"Where do they hunt and how much do they bring back?" Endre wondered aloud.

"They hunt in the surrounding area, taking a combination of livestock and humans in secluded areas," Gunnar recited. "It is enough to keep up our strength."

Endre's stomach roiled at the mention of the humans. He assumed any who were hunted did not survive.

"The Master has ordered us to keep our presence as unknown as possible," Gunnar continued. "We take the minimum we need to survive."

"How many is that? The minimum?" Endre asked, once again struck by just how much he did not know about the monster he had become. He did not even know how much or how often he needed to feed to survive. He imagined if left to it, he would find out very quickly.

"We have been bringing in just over one hundred humans a week," Gunnar told him, and Endre looked at him, aghast. One hundred lives lost to this horde outside of battle. But if he were honest with himself, he had expected more.

"We cannot sustain that," Endre whispered in a low tone so no others nearby could hear them. "We would decimate entire villages in mere weeks."

"Yes," Gunnar breathed, a look of concern passing over his face, "but what choice do we have? The men must feed."

Gunnar was, of course, right. The horde must be fed if they wanted to defend themselves against the other Vampires The Master spoke of.

"Can we shift to more livestock?" Endre asked.

"Livestock blood does not replenish like human blood does. Every man gets a combination of both to ensure he has fed enough to stave off the bloodlust, and also to make sure he gets human blood to keep up his strength," Gunnar whispered in reply, shaking his head.

"Is The Master aware of the attention we will start to draw if we continue at this pace?" Endre asked.

Gunnar nodded. "He has accelerated his plans now that you are here."

"I do not even know what his plans are," Endre lamented, feeling angry he was still in the dark.

"Nor do I," Gunnar stated. "I only know we have not seen this kind of movement for training until you arrived."

"Alright," Endre started, "we will begin training tomorrow. Perhaps then The Master will divulge his plans," he finished without hope.

Gunnar nodded his assent as a voice calling the Vampires to feed sounded through the camp. The back of Endre's throat burned with the need to feed, but he suddenly did not want to know how his dinner was going to be served.

CHAPTER EIGHT

Nearly a week had passed since The Master had given Endre his proclamation to train the troops. He strode to The Master's tent to give his report of the night's training endeavors. In the short time Endre had been in the camp, things began to feel normal. If he did not examine changes to sleeping when the sun shone instead of the moon, or being served blood from vats sitting next to piles of human and livestock carcasses, he could almost believe he was still employed in King Fairhair's army. He had developed a strong friendship with Gunnar and some of the other Vampires, though there were those who were suspicious of him and hostile when it was announced he would assume the post of Commander. All it took to cement his position as leader of the horde was a brutal lesson in combat with one of his detractors, which resulted in the other Vampire's body and head falling in separate directions after a strike of Endre's sword.

The Master had not been pleased Endre had reduced their numbers by one. The Master did, however, condone the use of the belligerent Vampire as an example to the remainder of the horde of what consequences awaited those who questioned Endre's position. That fateful event transpired on the first night of training. Endre had had no similar incidents since, though the looks of hatred from some continued. He could handle their sneers; the horde fearing and hating him was better than merely being hated and pegged as an easy target. Their fear kept Endre safe from retribution for felling their comrade—for the time being.

When Endre finished giving his report on the progress of the warriors, he was relieved to find The Master looked not only pleased but perhaps even impressed. Endre was satisfied with the progress the troops had made. He had never seen such strides in such a short amount of time. Some of the Vampires had barely known how to fight when they started on the field that first night, despite having been harvested from the dying on various battlefields. Now, every Vampire would pose a very real threat to any other Vampires that saw fit to attack them.

"Very good, you have passed your first test. It is time to introduce you to the second. Come with me," The Master said, rising to his feet and leaving the tent in a brisk walk.

Endre followed closely behind, growing more perplexed and wary with each step. After a few moments, they reached two soldiers holding the reins of a pair of horses. The Master mounted one of the beasts and gestured for Endre to do the same with the other horse. Endre obliged, struggling to contain his apprehension. The Master led his horse in a cantor Endre's mount quickly matched. Every few seconds, Endre glanced over at The Master, well aware of the cloak and dagger manner with which he was operating.

After they had traveled for some minutes, The Master reined his horse to a slow walk, and Endre did the same. Again, they traveled in silence, The Master giving nothing away to indicate his intentions. When the trees thinned out, revealing the edge of a craggy cliff, The Master pulled his steed to a stop. Endre steered his horse beside The Master's, mindful to keep at a distance where The Master could not reach him.

"Do you see them down there?" The Master asked, his eyes riveted on the ground at the base of the cliff.

Endre glanced to where The Master stared, surprised to find even at several land-miles away he could make out a small village quite clearly in the darkened night. The muted glow of fires illuminated the movement of the village's inhabitants, who Endre could plainly see consisted mostly of women and children. He could imagine their men had been called to King Fairhair's war, just as he had been, and he wondered how many of them lay dead with the crows picking at their bones.

"I do," Endre answered, as entranced by the scene of everyday life before them as The Master was.

"What do you see?" The Master asked, turning to survey Endre.

Endre kept his gaze on the village, not quite understanding what was being asked of him. Was he to assess their numbers? Their structures? Was he viewing them as a man? A soldier? A Vampire?

"A village. Houses," Endre stated, injecting false confidence into his tone.

"No, what are they?" The Master demanded, his tone belying impatience for Endre's obviously incorrect assessment.

"Women and children," Endre responded hesitantly.

"Wrong! They are animals. Livestock. Food," The Master spat with disdain. "You are new to this world, so I will forgive your oversight," he sneered. "You are no longer one of them. You can no longer count yourself among their ranks. You are a Vampire, and as such, those," he said, his voice impassioned as he pointed to the village, "are merely a resource. A commodity. It is written in the laws of nature that the strong prey upon the weak. We are the superior species. It is our right by nature to take our sustenance from them."

Endre ruminated on The Master's words for a moment, but it still did not make sense to him. He had never been considered a daft man, but trying to piece together the puzzle The Master attempted to place before him made him feel like one.

"There are those," The Master continued, "of our kind, though they are an embarrassment to the name Vampire, who view the humans differently. The Council. They wish to protect them. They would have all Vampires forsake nature and lock away our true selves. We were made to feast on the flesh and blood of the humans, but they see us as abominations. This horde, which you will lead, is not to fight the humans, it is to combat those Vampires who have betrayed us. The humans serve a dual purpose. They will feed our army and act as a beacon to draw our enemies to us. There we will face them in combat and decimate their ranks."

"But they are women and children," Endre whispered, a sense of dread flooding his entire being.

The Master moved too quickly for Endre to back his horse away and gripped Endre's jaw with a pressure very near to cracking the bone. Endre's face was wrenched to meet the fire in The Master's eyes as he felt the pressure of a blade at his chest.

"They are nothing more than food. These are the humans who take to hunting our kind. They must be eradicated, regardless of what sits between their legs. Once you have the scent of their blood in your lungs, you will no longer care about their age or sex. Was I mistaken in granting you this honor of immortality? In choosing you to lead my horde?" The Master hissed at him, his voice as much a threat as his words.

"No," Endre ground out around the pain in his jaw.

"Good. You will amass the Vampire horde tomorrow at sundown and raze that village to the ground," The Master ordered, releasing his grip on Endre's jaw and sheathing his sword.

The Master turned his horse and headed back toward camp, leaving Endre to stare at the village of innocent humans he was to decimate.

CHAPTER NINE

Endre tossed and turned during the sparse daylight hours, unable to quiet his mind enough to sleep. In a few short hours, The Master expected him to lead an attack on a village comprised solely of women and children. What bothered him more than the order was the fact the monster inside him churned with excitement at the prospect of so many fresh kills. He alternated between horror and anticipation for hours before he fell into a fitful sleep.

Endre walked through a forest strewn with bodies and stained with blood, his boots making squelching noises with each step. The warmth of the fallen men and their blood had thawed the ground enough to melt the light dusting of snow clinging to the dead grass. Overhead, carrion birds cawed and threatened him for getting too near their dinners, but he paid them no mind. Endre longed to look up at them perched in a long-dead tree, congregating in the last few moments of sunlight, but his neck would not turn as he commanded it.

The feeling was familiar to him now, and he understood that just as his dream several nights before had not been an ordinary dream and instead a blood memory, this one was as well. But he was not a woman in this dream; the strength and power with which he held himself spoke of a man—The Master.

The Master continued to walk through the field, taking Endre along as an unwilling participant in his memory. His head swung from side to side, taking in each of the fallen. He looked and listened for clues to find those still breathing and the ones worthy enough to join his horde of Vampires. There were few who still breathed here, though several faint heartbeats could be discerned from the ruckus of the flock perched in the trees above him. As he wove his way between the naked trees, following the sounds of life, the crows above followed him from tree to tree. He finally looked up, and what he saw could only be described as a dark omen. He had expected to see perhaps a few hundred of the birds watching him. He stopped for a moment and stared at them, his eyes scanning from tree to tree—assessing the murder gathering above—and estimated there were thousands observing him.

"I just want one," The Master's voice echoed in Endre's head with a chuckle. "You can have all the rest."

Endre's gut twisted with dread. He was about to see the transformation of one of his comrades. He had already lived through his own; he did not desire to experience it from The Master's perspective.

The crows cawed in answer, their collective voices echoing through the empty forest. The Master stepped over another dead body and was face-to-face with a dying Gunnar.

Endre tried to call out to his friend, warn him of his impending fate, but that was not how these dreams worked. What happened in these visions were past atrocities already carried out; there would be no saving Gunnar whose eyes were wild with fear and his breaths shallow, biding their time until they drew in their last.

"What are you?" Gunnar whispered, his voice coming out in a harsh rasp only death could create.

"Your Master," The Master said, and Endre could feel the corners of his mouth turn up in a smile.

Without even being able to see The Master's face, Endre knew it was the same smile which possessed a terrifying malevolence. Nausea ripped through Endre; he knew what came next, and there was nothing he could do to stop it. Endre was captive of The Master's memory, a puppet to carry out Gunnar's death against his will.

The Master cut across his wrist and brought it to Gunnar's lips, but Gunnar closed his mouth and turned away from the blood oozing from the cut. The Master grabbed Gunnar's face violently, wrenching his mouth open and eliciting a cry from the still-human version of Gunnar. Blood dripped into Gunnar's mouth as he struggled with all the energy remaining in his frail body to fight off the much stronger Vampire, but it was merely a practice in futility, as were Endre's efforts to fight the past. All at once, The Master pulled his wrist away and released Gunnar, leaving his face smeared with bright-red blood.

"I do not want to be a demon," Gunnar whispered when The Master placed his hands along both sides of Gunnar's head. Endre remembered the motion well and knew what was to come next.

"You are mine now. Welcome to my horde," The Master said, and snapped Gunnar's neck with one quick movement.

Endre watched in horror through the eyes of the murderer as his new friend lost his first life only to gain his second.

A gasp escaped Endre as he slipped back to the world of the present. Sucking in deep breaths to calm his racing heart, he attempted to clear the brutality of Gunnar's transition from his mind. It was particularly unnerving to have performed the ritual as the instrument of The Master. Endre shuddered and basked in the cool air on his sweat-soaked body.

"Was it a particularly gruesome one?" Gunnar asked as he lay beside Endre in their tent. Endre did not even bother to open his eyes to answer, unsure if he could bear the pain or the hatred he might see on Gunnar's face.

"It was yours," Endre admitted, knowing he did not have to specify what it was he had seen.

"I was the first of the horde," Gunnar said quietly.

Endre opened his eyes; he had not known. When they had first met, Gunnar had told him he had only been with the horde for two months. The picture started to look a little clearer. That meant the other Vampires, with the exception of The Master, were less than two months into this new life. It now made sense why there had been no commander before Endre, why the horde was still untrained. It also made sense they had gone undetected because it had been mere months since the inception of the army. When Endre had been forcibly enlisted, he had been under the impression the Vampire army had been in operation for years.

"How old is The Master?" Endre asked thoughtfully.

"It is not known, and I would not speak of it again," Gunnar warned.

Endre nodded and closed his eyes again. There was only an hour or so remaining until sundown, though he had no illusions he would sleep in that time. His entire body was energized—the same way he always felt before a battle—but this time it was different. This was not battle. This was slaughter. Those humans The Master intended to use as a beacon to draw out his enemies would not be able to fight them off. They were women and children. And even if those women were made of the same steel as the women he had known all his life, they would still be no match. Even if they had been seasoned men, they would all fall to the horde. The Master had said it plainly before: a Vampire could outfight humans one hundred to one, and that was with the assumption those they were fighting were hardened warriors. Endre had to find a way to prevent the upcoming massacre. He had become a monster in form, but he would not allow himself to become one in action if he could help it. And there were no guarantees once the scent of blood hit his nostrils the monster would not claw its way through his defenses.

"Gunnar," Endre whispered at a volume only his tent-mate could hear.

Gunnar's head turned toward him, his eyes shining with curiosity.

"We need to send out a warning to those humans, tell them to flee before nightfall," Endre said, trying to devise a plan.

"They will not get far," Gunnar warned. "Even if we warn them, they will not get far enough away that we could not catch them."

"We have to try. I am not a butcher," Endre hissed through gritted teeth.

"What would you have me do?" Gunnar asked helplessly.

"Are there any men you can trust? Men who do not see eye to eye with The Master's ways?" Endre asked, his voice pleading.

"There are a few," Gunnar said thoughtfully, rubbing at his beard.

"Send one," Endre ordered. "You cannot go. You would be missed."

Gunnar nodded and silently slipped from the tent. Endre hoped his footsteps through the camp would go unnoticed amongst the still-sleeping Vampires.

CHAPTER TEN

"Vampires!" The Master shouted, addressing the warriors gathered before him. "Tonight, we feast and wreak havoc on the humans! Their village will serve as their funeral pyre. Their destruction will draw our enemies to us so we may defeat them and live with the absolute freedom nature intended for her ultimate predator!"

Endre stood next to The Master as he addressed the massing of the troops. He looked from face to face, cataloging each of those who might join him in an attempt to overthrow The Master and put an end to his deranged plans, and those who would stand beside The Master and relish the destruction he wrought. His column of allies was significantly shorter than that of his enemies. If Endre wanted to stage a coup, he would be sorely outnumbered. He only hoped this phantom army The Master imagined their Vampires enemies possessed would assemble and rectify the imbalance in Endre's cataloging. Endre found Gunnar's face in the crowd, and his friend gave him a barely perceptible nod to acknowledge his task was done. Endre could only hope the villagers had taken heed of their warning and were land-miles away from their homes.

When The Master finished his speech, Endre mounted his horse and gave the order for his small-but-deadly contingent to follow him down the hillside to what they assumed was the unsuspecting village. The horde marched in relative silence, only the metallic jingles of buckles and the creak of leather accompanying their movement. Not a word was spoken as they made their way through the night.

As Endre neared the village, he scanned for movement—to his dismay, he saw quite a bit of it. Either their message had not been received, or it had not been heeded. He held up his hand to halt the troops, stalling in an attempt to devise a backup plan to save the people moving about before him. A chorus of murmurs rose up behind him, the other Vampires impatient with his hesitation. The Master could not know of it; he would be dead before he returned to the camp and all his plans of stopping The Master's carnage would disappear with his second death.

Endre turned to face his troops again, fixing a gruesome smile which reflected his dread, not his intentions. "Burn it to the ground," he told them, his gaze stopping on those he knew were his allies, the pleading clear in his eyes. Spare them, he communicated.

A war cry rose around him, and his horse trailed the mass of Vampires as they raced toward the village, the Vampires moving faster than his horse. Endre arrived in the village moments after his warriors, and already they had caused destruction. His horse wove around Vampires huddled over their kill, draining the bodies. When Endre reached the middle of the village, several of the buildings were ablaze and screams filled the air. One of the horde bellowing in agony drew his attention, and he turned his horse in the direction of the tormented sounds. Tearing between buildings, Endre dodged humans as they fled from their houses, paying them no mind as they made way for him. Focusing on the smell of singed flesh and screams for mercy, Endre drew them into his being and held them there. They served as an anchor to the reality about him when his demon roared from within, demanding admission to the slaughter. He continued to deny it entry, forcing away the gnawing need for the blood all around him.

When Endre passed between two buildings to the source of the cry, he saw Gunnar on his knees, an arrow protruding from his chest. One of the women of the village stood, sword in hand, ready to strike off Gunnar's head. Endre bounded from his horse and put himself between Gunnar and the blade, blocking the swing with his arm. He hissed as the blade slid through his skin, slicing the flesh and drawing blood. The woman took a step back in shock, surprised at his sudden appearance. An arrow shot past his head so narrowly missing him, he could feel the tip of one of the feathers brush his cheek as it flew past.

"Run!" the woman shouted, taking a defensive stance against Endre.

Endre growled and lunged at the woman, intent on removing the sword from her hands.

"You should not be here. You should have left!" Endre barked at her, dodging when she swung at him.

"We would never fall for your ruse, Vampire." She spat the last word. "We know the tricks of your kind: lure us from our defenses, scatter us in the dark woods, and take us out one by one."

She punctuated each of her points with slashes of her sword much faster than a human should be capable of. Had the horde actually infiltrated a Vampire settlement, unbeknownst to them? That could not be right, not with the way her words dripped with venom when she spoke of his kind. She was quick, but she was still not as fast as him.

"What are you?" Endre asked, as he blocked one of her blows with his blade and dodged another arrow aimed for his head.

He had intended to save these people, direct them away from harm, and now he was fighting for his survival. A crowd of Vampires filed between the buildings, one of them taking out the villager who continued to send a barrage of arrows at him. The woman screamed as one of Endre's horde plunged his fangs into her neck.

"No!" the warrior woman screamed, her attention diverted from the fight before her to her fallen comrade.

Endre took the opportunity to strike. The woman grimaced when his blade caught along her side. The scent of her blood flooded his senses, clouding his judgment, calling to his demon. His thoughts merged to the single-minded purpose of tasting her blood. The woman pressed one hand along her wound and continued to fight, but he barely registered her defense. His eyes were instead riveted on the growing pool of red spreading beneath her hand. Endre took deep breaths, trying to keep the demon within at bay, but he could not take his eyes from the crimson stain underneath her fingers.

The woman lunged at him, her form sloppy and her body much too close. Endre reached out and grasped the wrist of her sword hand, and she cried out in pain as he squeezed, grinding the bones together. Her weapon dropped to the dirt at her feet, and she collapsed to her knees. Endre yanked her toward him, and she let out a cry of distress at his rough handling. He dropped his own sword and used his free hand to grasp her throat, his limbs moving as if of their own accord, surrendering to the siren scent of her blood.

"I tried to warn you. I tried to save you," Endre whispered, kneeling with her in his arms before the darkness enveloped him completely from the inside. "I tried, I cannot," he said, hearing his agony echoed in his words.

The woman's eyes grew wide at his confession. "Just do not bring me back," she said with tears in her eyes.

"I will not," Endre promised with the last vestiges of the control to which he clung before the demon consumed him completely and he plunged his fangs into her neck.

The woman let out a cry of pain, and Endre answered with his own moan of pure bliss. How could he fight this? Undiluted euphoria flooded his entire being as he took in mouthful after mouthful of her blood. It tasted different than the other woman he had sampled—it was sweeter. He had sampled the unsullied woman in The Master's tent when he had first arrived, and though her flavor was better than any culinary wonder he had ever experienced, this woman's far surpassed that. Endre drew from her until her body went limp in his arms. When he pulled his fangs from her flesh, he dropped her body to the dirt and looked around for more. He needed more. Whatever these villagers were, their blood was like a delicacy to the Vampires.

Endre stalked from building to building, searching for heartbeats and snuffing them out. He glutted himself on blood, losing track of the number of lives he claimed. The buildings burned around him, but he continued on in bloodlust, taking from the women and the elderly around him until a blade slipped through his ribcage from behind, halting his rampage. Endre roared in pain and anger, the entire length of the blade scraping along his flesh as it was drawn from his body. When he turned to face his attacker—the coward who could only strike him down from behind—he was met with the face of one of his fiercest enemies amongst the horde.

"I will tell them one of these weak humans killed you. Your name will go hand in hand with shame," the Vampire snarled at him. Endre had never bothered to learn his name.

Endre dodged his next blow but had no weapon of his own, having dropped it in the dirt next to the body of his first victim of the night. The other Vampire caught him with the blade again, this time perilously close to his heart. He twisted the blade with a maniacal laugh as Endre roared with pain. But he did not intend to go out without taking this one with him. Endre pushed forward, easing the blade further into his chest, the pressure catching his breath. The Vampire looked at him in wide-eyed surprise having not foreseen Endre's intentions. Endre darted his head forward, sending sharp pangs through his chest, attacking his assailant with his last remaining weapon. His jaw locked around the Vampire's neck and Endre reared back, ripping out his opponent's throat, spitting it at his feet.

The wounded Vampire clasped his throat, trying to stem the rampaging torrent of blood spilling forth. In one swift movement, Endre drew the sword from his chest, the blade slicing the palms of his hands. With one well-placed swing, he cut through the remainder of the Vampire's neck and watched with grim satisfaction as his head rolled across the floor, thumping against a wall with a sickening smack.

Endre dropped to his knees, clasping both hands over his chest, his attempt to slow the blood flow an exercise in futility. In the back of his mind, he knew the blade had nicked his heart when it had been twisted; there was no hope for survival. In his time training the Vampire horde, he had learned there were two ways to kill a Vampire: severing the head from body, or piercing the heart. It would seem the second method would do him in. His breath grew shallow and he eased onto his back. It made sense the gods would see fit he should die a second time in nearly the same position as the first. Though where there were birds and the sky before, now there was only flame and smoke. As he searched above him for the sky, he noticed for the first time the building around him was engulfed in flames. At least he would have a funeral pyre.

CHAPTER ELEVEN

Endre tested his opponent with a practice swing of his sword. She was good, but so was he. They traded a flurry of strikes, the girl across from him smiling and jeering with each swing.

"Thyra, where is this thunder you are supposed to possess?" the girl who spun around for a swing taunted.

Endre recognized a blood memory; this one was from one of the women he had fed off in the village attack. He could not discern which one, considering his bloodlust had taken over and he had lost track of the tally of victims.

Thyra blocked the blow and delivered one of her own, sending the other girl off balance. Thyra tripped the girl and she went sprawling to the ground. Thyra's blade was at the girl's throat, and with the tiniest flick of her wrist, she gave her a small cut, just barely enough to draw blood.

"Here it is," Thyra's voice echoed in Endre's head. She lowered her blade and reached out to help the girl up. The two embraced, and Endre could detect no malice between them. It seemed it was a training exercise, similar to what he had performed with his Vampire horde—but with less ego.

"Well done, girls, time for your lesson with the elders," a woman spoke from behind them as she ushered them into a building.

"Ugh," Thyra's opponent groaned. "They bore me."

"I like them," Thyra said, bumping into her friend playfully.

"Girls," a sharp voice said, drawing their attention. An elderly woman gestured for the two girls to sit. "Erika, do you know why we teach you to fight like the men?" the woman asked, addressing the girl Thyra had been practicing against.

"So we can protect ourselves," Erika answered solemnly.

"Correct. Who else do we protect?" the old woman continued her barrage of questions.

"Humans," Erika answered, her eyes lighting up.

"Do not forget it is our responsibility to protect against the Vampires, both humans and our own Hunters alike," the elder reminded with a shake of her finger.

Endre listened with rapt attention, hoping to glean some information about this new species, as well as the population he had become a part of. But was he still part of it? The last he remembered, he was lying mortally wounded in a burning building. He dragged his attention away from his own thoughts and back to the memory playing before him, but it had begun to fade. He grasped in vain at the memory, trying to pull himself back into it, but he had no control over it and lost it completely, only to be enveloped in pure blackness.

Endre breathed in ash and soot, the foreign matter burning as it clung to the inside of his organs. He tried to open his eyes, but it felt as though a heavy weight lay on them. With another attempt, he pried them open but was met with darkness; even his Vampire eyesight had trouble making anything out. He tried to rub at the grit stinging his eyes, but his arms were pinned beside him. With frantic movements, he was able to move one of his arms, the sound of crashing around him meeting his ears. He lay in the rubble of the collapsed building, the weight of it crushing down on him, trapping him in place. Pulling on his other arm, Endre managed to dislodge enough debris to allow sunlight to filter through the gaps. He gasped at the bright light, having not experienced sunlight in its most direct form since his transformation. The brightness burned his eyes, so he closed them quickly. He would not need his eyes to dig out of these ruins.

After several long minutes of shifting his limbs and dislodging the stone and charred lumber which buried him, Endre had managed to free himself. His hands first found the wound at his chest, the wound that should have killed him. He ran his fingers through the cut in the fabric of his shirt and over where the blade had been lodged. There was nothing. Not even a scar. He had sustained a few injuries in the training fields, but never one so dire as the one he had thought would take his life. Each of those smaller wounds healed quickly, but he did not expect this one to do the same. He ascribed the small miracle to his gluttonous consumption of blood during the massacre.

Shame flooded him as he thought about the control he had lost and the lives he had taken when his intention was to save them. His second death would have been penance for his lack of strength of will, but it seemed the gods still had a use for him. What would he do now? He could not stomach the thought of returning to the horde; he had no place there. This was his way out. He would be presumed dead, fallen in the fight. He could go home.

Endre choked out a sob when he thought about home, about his wife, Ingrid. There had not been a single hour of daylight when Endre had not thought about her. In those first days, he thought about leaving and going to her, but The Master would never simply allow him to go. He would have been hunted like an animal and slaughtered for his desertion, and if he ever made it back to Ingrid, she would have been, too. Now that threat was lifted. But what would she think of what he had become? He had to believe their love was strong enough to overcome and they would find a way to forge ahead and live out the future they had always dreamed of together.

Dust and debris poured off him as he clamored to his feet. It would be a long journey on foot, but every step that brought him closer to his beloved Ingrid would be worth it. Endre shielded his eyes from the sun and got his bearings. He was going home.

"Commander?" Gunnar's voice interrupted Endre's thoughts.

That simple word alone dashed the hopes of seeing his wife. How could he have thought he could escape the horde? Endre turned slowly to his friend. Gunnar stood with a frown, taking in Endre's soot-stained, tattered clothing.

"We thought you had fallen," Gunnar commented, the furrow between his brows still present.

"I did. I have," Endre answered.

There was still hope to leave the service of The Master. Gunnar was the only Vampire he could see or hear in the vicinity. He trusted Gunnar would not bar his path, should he choose to continue homeward. And if he did, Endre could not claim he was not desperate enough to harm Gunnar and flee anyway.

"I cannot stay here," Endre explained, his eyes pleading with Gunnar to understand. "I must go home. To my wife," he continued, his voice breaking with emotion when he spoke of her.

Gunnar glanced about him, searching for watching eyes or listening ears. "Go," he said with a heavy sigh. "The Master assumes you are dead, I see no reason to tell him otherwise. Go to your wife and cherish the fortune the gods have bestowed upon you."

He placed a heavy hand on Endre's shoulder and squeezed it. It was as close as they would come to an embrace. Gunnar reached into the ashes at Endre's feet and pulled first Endre's sword, then a broken and charred bit of his shield. Gunnar pressed the sword into Endre's hand and held the broken piece of shield between them.

"Proof of death," Gunnar explained. He then pulled the fur cloak from around his shoulders and draped it across Endre's. "Keep warm, my friend. Do not come back," he warned with a low tone and a shake of his head.

"Thank you," Endre answered graciously with a bow. "Until we meet in Valhalla."

"I'll save you a seat," Gunnar answered grimly, his face breaking into a sad smile.

Gunnar was a better man than Endre could ever hope to be. He put his life on the line allowing Endre to walk away from the horde, knowing full well the consequences should The Master uncover his betrayal. Endre liked to believe he would have done the same, but a man never knew the true stock he was made of until forced into a situation where he had to thoroughly examine it.

Endre turned his back on a Vampire he trusted with his life and hoped it was many years before they met again—either in this lifetime or the next.

CHAPTER TWELVE

After a walk that should have lasted weeks as a human, Endre stood at the doorstep of his home. It had been a mere three days since clawing himself from the wreckage of the collapsed building. He looked down at his body, deeming himself presentable to see his wife. He had stopped at a nearby stream and washed the blood and grime from his body and clothing, giving him a new start.

As he stood outside, debating the first words he would speak to his wife after nearly a year since he'd left to wage war, noises from inside caught his attention. He listened closely; the sounds he heard were both familiar and foreign to him. He heard his wife's moans and the slapping of flesh against flesh, those sounds he knew well from the times they had made love. The sound of a man and his rapid breathing paired with whispered words that would have reddened his sweet wife's cheeks were alien to him. Not wanting to see what he knew lay beyond the door, he stood on the threshold trying to control the rage threatening to take over. An especially loud moan sounded from his wife, and he could hold back no longer.

Endre entered his home, the home he had built with his own hands. He was greeted by the sight of one of his former comrades in arms thrusting into his wife. Ingrid saw him first and her eyes went wide with shock, or fear, Endre could not tell which it was. Perhaps both.

"Stop!" she yelled at her lover, beating her fist on his chest. He merely took her hands in his and pressed them into the bed without breaking pace. "You have to stop!" Ingrid screamed at him again.

Her shouts were drowned out by the man's elongated moan as he emptied himself inside Ingrid. His wife. Endre strode to the bed and pulled the man from his wife. The sight of his seed dripping from her threw him into a red rage. Before the man could register who Endre was, or the murderous look on his face, he was dead on the floor, his neck broken.

Endre's gaze went back to his wife still lying on the bed half exposed and frozen in terror, her mouth open in a silent scream. Endre still did not know what he was going to do with her. Did his love for her outweigh her betrayal? He took a step toward the bed, his movement spurring her own. Ingrid scrambled from the bed and ran to the door.

Endre was there in a heartbeat before she could pull it open, his palm against the wood preventing her escape. She tugged at the door and gave a little whimper when it would not budge. Her frantic movements sent a cloud of her scent rolling over Endre, and his anger dissipated with his need for her. She was his life, his reason for living.

"Ingrid," he whispered into her ear, his nose nuzzling along her neck. Her familiar scent was like a balm to his soul, soothing his shame and guilt away.

"You are dead," she whispered to the door, her body trembling in fear.

"I am here. I came back for you," he told her, brushing her long hair over her shoulder so he could kiss her neck.

He started behind her ear and made his way to her exposed shoulder. It did not matter to him she had just been with another man. He wanted her. He missed her. He needed to be inside her. He needed to be home. He gently grasped her shoulders and turned her so he could look into her mossy-green eyes he loved so much. He could see a million worlds and a million different futures whenever he looked into them.

"You are a ghost, come back to haunt me," Ingrid said in a quavering voice.

"It is me, Ingrid. It is your husband," Endre pleaded, taking her chin in his palm to hold her gaze.

She squeezed her eyes tightly closed, refusing to meet his eyes. "Leave here, demon," she pleaded. "I will take no part in your wicked ways!"

"Ingrid. Ingrid," Endre pleaded, but she still would not look at him. "Look at me!" he roared, and her eyes popped open, widening when they met his eyes.

"You are a demon!" she cried, pushing against him.

Endre struggled to hold her, to pull her into his embrace, but she continued to push against him. His chest tightened with anguish. This is not how he'd envisioned his homecoming and their reunion. He buried his face into the neck of his struggling wife, drawing in her scent, willing her to see that though he was different, it was still him.

Her heart beat frantically, her pulse a living thing where his face was pressed. Endre attempted to ignore the panicked pace, but it spoke to something more primitive inside him. He tried to suppress the voice that called to him to silence the heartbeat, but the monster's voice was loud and insistent. It was only her heartbeat, and all other sound around him ceased to exist. Her struggle and cries went unnoticed as his focus was solely aimed where her blood pulsed through the artery at her neck. Soon, hearing it was not enough; he had to see it, had to see the way the skin on her neck jumped with every push of blood through her heart.

Endre pulled his head away from Ingrid's warm skin and brushed her hair aside so he could watch. The sight of the pulse in her neck was hypnotic, luring him further and further away from rationality. He had to taste her. Just one taste. He grasped her chin with one hand and tilted her head back. Yes, that was it. The thrumming of life beneath her creamy flesh was beautiful. He ran his tongue along the pulsing vessel, feeling the flow of blood just beneath the surface. One taste would not be enough. He wanted it all.

Endre sank his fangs into Ingrid's neck, silencing her scream with a hand, squeezing to cut off her supply of air. Her frail fists struck out at him, and he had to keep from laughing at her feeble attempt to resist him. She deserved this. She had betrayed him. She had taken another man into her bed—into their bed—and then denied him. Endre continued to drink. After a few moments, he tried to convince himself to stop, tried to remind himself although she deserved to be punished, she did not deserve death. He still loved her. He would always love her, even though she could not love the monster he had become. His bloodlust refused to heed his pleas to spare her life, and he continued to drink. Soon, her movements slowed and eventually stopped, her body sagging into his.

He pulled off Ingrid's neck by sheer force of will, but it was already too late. Her vibrant heartbeat was gone, replaced with deathly silence. Endre looked down at the body of his beloved with a mixture of disgust and regret.

"Ingrid!" Endre howled in pain, clutching her body to his chest.

His pain was quickly replaced by satisfaction, having fed his needs. He pushed away at the momentary contentment, needing to feel the shame, the guilt, the overwhelming revulsion he had for himself. He was a monster, borne straight from the depths of Hel, and wherever he went, he wrought misery.

Alarmed shouting from outside drew him from his brief moment of wallowing. Others would have heard the screams and would be on their way to investigate. He knew he had to leave if he did not want to die a second time, though he debated staying to face the fate he surely deserved. That the Norns could be so cruel was never more evident than at the moment when he looked upon his lifeless wife, drained away by the demon he had become. Running footsteps drew closer to the house; they were almost upon him. Endre was out of time. If faced with peril, the monster within him would rear its ugly head, taking more innocent lives with him before he perished. He could not stay.

The decision made, Endre threw open the door moments before his fellow villagers arrived. Gasps and shouts of anger sounded behind him as he ran with all his strength into the nearby woods. He did not yet know where he would go, but his instincts told him to get as far away as possible.

CHAPTER THIRTEEN

Endre wandered through the woods of his ancestral homeland, taking in every tree and stone he would have to leave and never return to. Dawn was quickly approaching, and although he could make the journey in daylight if he kept to the cover of the bare canopy, he was exhausted, despite having fed so recently. It was the subject of his most recent feeding that left his mind weary and his heart heavy. He needed a place to rest until twilight once again blanketed the world.

Endre made his way to a cave he had known as a child. It was once the home of a fearsome bear that was the subject of many tales in his home village, but the bear had long since passed on to another world, even if his legends still remained in this one. As Endre crawled his way through the opening into the darkness, he had the distinct feeling of being a demon trying to claw its way back to the underworld. Surely, Hel was where he belonged, but he would have to find another path to get there.

Endre evaluated his options as he settled into the darkness. The only person he had had left in the world had been violently torn out of it by his own hands. He was a murderer, and now his only home was both empty and forbidden to him. Was he cursed to roam the world, unleashing the creature within to feed off innocent humans like his dear, sweet Ingrid? In his mind, even such an existence as that looked bleak with only the promise of death and destruction wherever he went.

Right now, he could have been in Valhalla instead. He could have been escorted to the Hall of Heroes among the Valkyries, awaiting his turn to fight for the gods in the great battle of Ragnarok. Now, he imagined he would be fighting on the opposing side when the Great War came. He was not naïve enough to believe the gods would take a demon such as him into their army to fight against his own ilk. A wave of self-loathing and pity rolled over him. Endre was cursed to walk the earth as an untamed, bloodthirsty beast because The Master wanted a Vampire army. This was all the fault of The Master.

The final thought sent anger surging through Endre. The Master was to blame for all of this. It was he who'd created the monster Endre had become. Without his interference, Endre would be dining in the Hall of Heroes with his fellow fallen warriors, not preying on humans. If it had not been for The Master, Ingrid would still be alive, and Endre convinced himself he could have even stomached the thought of her being with another man as long as her heart still beat. In the early hours of daylight, Endre decided the only way to go was back. He would go back to the horde and find a way to stop The Master from creating more monsters like him and destroying many more lives.

When darkness fell once again, Endre began his journey to where the Vampire army had last been camped. He did not know what he would find when he arrived. As far as he could tell from his time among the horde, they had not moved camp once they had established that location. The Master would venture with a few Vampires to the newest battle of King Fairhair's war and take his pick of the fallen warriors while the bulk of the army stayed behind. But The Master's latest campaign was not one to bolster his horde's numbers; it was an endeavor to catch the attention of his enemies. Endre did not know if the camp would still be occupied when he returned to it, or if his fellow Vampires would be marched off to meet the enemy in battle.

Endre should have known The Master was not of sound mind when he had heard his strategy. He should have known as soon as he'd learned The

Master was building an army of creatures borne from the very depths of Hel that he needed to be stopped. For all The Master's talk of the laws of nature, it was as though he did not understand them at all. There was a cycle to nature: birth, life, and death. That which had died could not live again. It was against the very laws of nature The Master was so fond of using as evidence to support his ambitions to lord over humans. The Vampires in and of themselves were against nature. They were abominations. He was an abomination. The only way Endre could see to reconcile the imbalance the Vampires created in the world of the living was to remove them from it, himself included.

As Endre made his journey over the span of several days, he also made his plans. The Master and the horde of Vampires needed to be stopped. He would fight until his last stolen breath to right the balance.

CHAPTER FOURTEEN

From his vantage point, Endre could see The Master's Vampire horde was still in place at the encampment. He had half expected them to have moved on by now, but he should have known The Master's arrogance would only allow for his enemies to seek him out. He would not go to them. It was to his advantage to draw them toward where he held his stronghold; he knew the terrain better than his enemies did. Endre could also see there was a small grouping of Vampires—presumably not from The Master's horde—approaching from the west. They were still far enough away even the scouts in the rotation Endre himself had set would not detect them yet.

A great battle raged within Endre. He longed to go to The Master, reincorporate himself into the horde, and dismantle it from the inside. But another part of him whispered to go to the approaching Vampires and seek their guidance. If they did not immediately capture or kill him on sight, perhaps he could convince them he was on the same side they were. There was also the risk the group was merely a small detachment sent from The Master to patrol the area to watch for signs of the enemy. At that point, Endre would be questioned on his whereabouts as well as his allegiances should he not return immediately to camp and make his survival known to The Master. If it was a contingent from The Master's horde and they were hostile, it was likely they would attempt to kill him. He knew, however, his fighting abilities exceeded theirs and he would fight to his last if he had to.

Endre decided to take the risk. He walked toward the group of riders, their horses meeting him outside the range of The Master's scouts. The mounts reared up as Endre appeared quickly in front of them, but their riders had already dismounted with weapons drawn. Endre studied the figures before him and was surprised to find both male and female Vampires before him. It had not even occurred to him there might be females of this species.

As the first of the males attacked him, Endre dodged, not having a weapon of his own to either block or return the attack. He held his hands up to show he was unarmed, unsure of what kind of honor these Vampires may possess and if they would adhere to such niceties of warfare. He could not say if his own horde would do so. The Vampire that attacked came to a standstill, no longer attacking but also refusing to lower his weapon. He pointed it at Endre's neck, ready to strike his head from his body should Endre make a false move against him.

"Are you a messenger?" the Vampire asked, his expression puzzled.

"No, but I do have a message," Endre replied with a smile.

"We do not have the time for riddles. Speak plainly or die where you stand," one of the females spoke up from beside her mount.

Endre looked her over, admiring the regal way with which she held herself. He was no stranger to seeing maidens as warriors, but seeing a Vampire one was a novelty to him.

"Take your eyes off my mate, or I will remove them for you," one of the attending males hissed, directing Endre's attention to him. "Now, speak your message before I remove your tongue."

Endre nodded solemnly. These were fierce warriors, but where they were more advanced in skill than The Master's army, they were sorely lacking in numbers. They would need the element of surprise, or at least knowledge of what they faced, before they could consider walking into an even match.

"And to whom am I delivering my message?" Endre asked with a small bow. These warriors intrigued him.

The Vampire who held a sword level with his neck advanced on him, lifting his arm to swing back and take Endre's head. He stopped mid-swing when the female who had addressed Endre earlier lifted her hand.

"Be still, Agmundr. Though impetuous, I admire his tenacity to ensure his message is delivered to the correct recipients. We have not yet been properly introduced. This is Agmundr," she said, gesturing to the Vampire ready to steal Endre's second life. "My mate is Egill." She gestured to the Vampire who'd threatened to remove first Endre's eyes and then his tongue. "And I am Magnhildr. The remainder of our entourage will be introduced to you should you live beyond the delivery of your message."

"Are you friend or foe to The Master?" Endre asked, suddenly wondering if perhaps he had run into allies for The Master.

"We have come to negotiate the terms of a truce with the one you call The Master, to cease his hostilities against the humans in this area," Magnhildr replied, narrowing her eyes at Endre.

"He will not cease," Endre thought aloud before he could stop himself.

Endre knew beyond a doubt there would be no truce and no cease in hostilities. They had been unwittingly lured into a cleverly laid trap by The Master.

"If that is the conclusion of your message," Magnhildr began, "then we are no longer in need of your services. Your head sent back to your master will be response enough."

Endre held his hands up in surrender once more. "Wait!" he urged. "The Master has no intention of ceasing hostilities or engaging in a truce with you. You have been lured here under false pretenses. Are you aware of how many Vampires his horde numbers?"

A chorus of murmurs went through the group of riders before Magnhildr held up her hand to silence them. "Horde?" she asked, genuine curiosity coloring her tone.

"Yes, horde," Endre replied adamantly as a sword point broke the skin on his neck.

"And what do you know of this horde, messenger?" Magnhildr asked.

"I know before the attack on the village not far from here, it numbered eighty-seven," Endre spoke quickly.

A murmur of dissent rolled through the riders, and once again Magnhildr silenced it with a wave of her hand.

"Lies!" Egill protested before Magnhildr could continue her interrogation.

"How many does it number now?" Magnhildr asked.

"We lost several Vampires in the village," Endre continued.

"We?" Magnhildr asked urgently, her eyes full of fury as they bored into him. Endre realized his mistake was associating himself with the group of Vampires these riders were here to defend the humans against.

"Kill him," Egill insisted, and the riders behind him nodded in agreement.

"Be still," Magnhildr sighed in exasperation. "It seems our messenger has valuable information for us. Your life depends on your continued cooperation. Continue to answer my questions truthfully and we may let you live. How did the humans kill several Vampires?"

"I do not believe they were human. They were Vampire Hunters of some kind," Endre answered, acutely aware of the blade that had pushed farther into his skin, threatening to spill more of his blood.

"How do you know this?" Magnhildr asked.

"I saw it," Endre hesitated, afraid to admit exactly how he had seen it and incriminate himself as a participant in the massacre.

"In a blood dream?" Magnhildr asked.

"Yes," Endre answered, his shame nearly palpable.

"Are you a deserter?" she asked.

"They thought I fell in the fight with the villagers. A burning building collapsed on me, I was left for dead," Endre said, shaking his head. He had left the horde, but they had left him to die first.

"When you awoke, which I assume you did as you are standing before us now, why did you not return to the horde?" she asked.

"I …" Endre started and paused. How did he tell them he was ashamed for what he had done? That he had taken his abandonment as a chance to live out his life and went back to his wife, only to have their reunion end in tragedy? "They left me to die. When I awoke, I took the opportunity to leave my indentured servitude in The Master's army and thought I could return to my old life. My old home," he continued. He was sure her next question would be why he was in limbo between the horde and his old life.

"Where is the horde now?" Magnhildr asked in a soft voice, drawing Endre's attention back to her face. She had presented a strong warrior façade to him, but Endre could see his own pain reflected in her eyes.

"We are outside the range of the scouts that patrol the perimeter outside the encampment,"

Endre divulged. "There are a dozen Vampires on patrol at any given time. Maybe more since the attack on the village. I have not dared get close enough for further reconnaissance."

"And why should we believe the information you provide?" Egill asked.

"Because he is a monster that must be stopped," Endre whispered, his gaze focusing on the night sky above them.

"Taste his blood, it will tell us the truth of things," Agmundr proclaimed, piercing the skin on Endre's neck and letting loose several new droplets of blood. Endre hissed at the intrusion of the steel, but otherwise made no move to pull himself from its path.

Magnhildr nodded her agreement. "It is the best way to determine where your loyalties lie," she stated, striding forward.

The three Vampires he had been introduced to approached him from different sides, as if he were a stag being cornered by wolves preparing for the kill. Endre stood still at their approach, hoping allowing them to see into his blood would be viewed as a show of good faith and cooperation. Agmundr made a fresh cut over the wound that had already sealed closed, the bite of his blade carrying an unnecessary malice. Each of the three swiped a finger through the droplets of crimson and brought

Endre's blood to their lips. Three sets of eyes dropped closed, and Endre could see the rapid movement of their eyes behind the lids.

After a moment of prolonged silence, the three Vampires opened their eyes in unison, each looking at the other in turn, as if communicating only with their gazes.

"Your blood has revealed many secrets," Magnhildr whispered conspiratorially. "We know your loss and your inner turmoil. We know what intentions are in your heart and your mind. We seek to aid you in your quest to destroy The Master, but your campaign ends with his death. We will not allow you to continue with your plans of destruction to Vampires beyond The Master's horde. If you choose to continue down that path, your second life is forfeit. Do you consent to relinquish your plans of genocide?"

Endre nodded, in awe they had seen so much in a tiny drop of blood. He had only experienced the blood memories sporadically, and then they were thrust upon his dreams, unbidden. It seemed these Vampires could summon them in their waking hours and pore through them all at once.

"Then it has been decided. In exchange for your cooperation in defeating the villain known as The Master, The Council has determined once the deed is done, your life shall remain your own," Magnhildr announced.

"The Council?" Endre asked.

"The Council is comprised of the three of us who stand before you," Magnhildr clarified. "Come, I believe we have some strategy to discuss," she said, walking to her horse and mounting it.

CHAPTER FIFTEEN

Endre sat across from Magnhildr in a tent similar to the one he had occupied with Gunnar not that long ago. He wondered briefly if Gunnar had survived the battle in the village. His thoughts were cut short when Egill cleared his throat. Endre jolted to attention, having realized while deep in thought, it must have looked as though he had been staring at the female. She chuckled, but did not look offended.

"We have seen The Master has spoken to you of The Council. However, his description of our role was inaccurate. He painted us as tyrants intending to suppress the Vampires. This is untrue," Magnhildr began. "A more accurate description of our purpose is to keep the balance. But it is not the same balance of life and death you presume I speak of. That balance will always be tipped in our favor. We have cheated death by our very existence, and we must take lives to continue ours. We do not make life. Vampires do not breed and only multiply by reclaiming the dead. I refer now to the balance between Vampires living in the shadows and exposure to humans."

Endre leaned forward in rapt attention. This was more information about his origins than he had ever hoped The Master would reveal to him. He knew so little about the world of Vampires and he intended to absorb any knowledge The Council wished to impart upon him.

"It is out of necessity we must live among the dark, remaining hidden from human eyes … a necessity some see as unfortunate and wish to change. It cannot. The balance is a delicate one, poised on the edge of a blade. If we remain so hidden we avoid contact with the humans altogether, we die. If we expose ourselves to them by open hostilities, we run the risk of eradication. The Master assumed the village to be an easy target, yet you have seen there are those who hunt our kind. Therefore, we must live in stealth for our own preservation," she told him, pausing to gauge his reaction. When Endre made no move to interrupt, she continued. "Though our motives may differ, we have the same outcome in mind. The Master must be stopped. He is a menace and his horde must be dissolved."

"How do you propose we accomplish this? Your numbers are no match for his. If you faced him in open battle, your entire entourage would be slaughtered. I have trained these Vampires myself, I know what they are capable of," Endre said, shaking his head. "Have you reinforcements on the way?"

"No, there is no one else coming to fight this battle," Magnhildr replied steadily. "We operate alone. The network of other Vampires out in the world is small, and communication with them becomes difficult when we strive to hide so well. Those we have been able to contact have refused to engage in the fight."

"Then your campaign is doomed," Endre said, defeated.

"It is not," Magnhildr said with a sly smile. "We have you."

"Me?" Endre asked doubtfully. The smile she gave him did not make him uneasy like The Master's signature one, but it certainly gave him no comfort.

"Yes. The only reason you are part of this meeting rather than lying in two pieces beside the path we met upon is because you are of use to us," she said, holding up her hand to stay the inevitable words of protest or indignation she knew he would utter. "It is a matter of preservation. If your motives had been anything other than the desire to stop The Master and destroy his army, we would not have let you live. Quite simply, we are in a position where we can help each other attain our goals. At the heart, they are one and the same: to stop The Master and his horde."

"I ask again, how is it you propose we do that with naught but ten Vampires against at least eight times that number?" Endre asked, folding his arms across his chest and leaning back in his chair.

He'd had three days to plan his assault on The Master as he walked from his home back to the encampment. His plan had been a suicide mission, having no hope of emerging from the confrontation alive. He expected after he claimed The Master's head he would be struck down by the guards or others loyal to The Master.

"We infiltrate from the inside," Magnhildr said with a triumphant smile.

"That is my role?" Endre scoffed.

"It is the same as you had planned all along, is it not?" Magnhildr asked with raised eyebrows.

"Aye, it was. But what is your part to play?" Endre asked skeptically.

"We will serve as reinforcements," she replied.

"You mean you will watch from the sidelines while I undertake a mission where the odds of me surviving are next to none. You did not take my life because you hope The Master's Vampires will do the work for you," Endre said with a nod of understanding.

"A traitor will always be a traitor," Egill hissed beside him. "You have turned on The Master, what says you will not turn on The Council once the threat of The Master and his horde is gone?"

"I was never loyal to The Master," Endre argued. "I performed the task he gave in order to survive."

"And you killed for him," Egill taunted.

"No, not for him. Blood memories do not show all. Did they show you I tried to warn the village and send its inhabitants away?" Endre asked, and when no one made a move to acknowledge or deny it, he continued, his voice impassioned, "I sent a messenger, but the villagers refused and stayed to fight. Surely the memories of my blood showed you I did not simply attack the humans in the village. I will not deny the monster within took hold, and yes, I did take lives. But never for him. I never swore fealty to The Master. I hold loyalty only to myself."

Magnhildr held up her hand to silence both Endre and Egill. "We may all perish in this fight," she stated, "such is the way of war. Surely, a warrior like yourself does not fear his own death?"

"It is not death I fear. I have done that already. It is the idea of being used as a pawn I fear," Endre said, narrowing his eyes at her.

"Enough bickering," Agmundr ordered, his voice cutting through the tension that had gathered in the tent. "Yes, there are ten, eleven counting you," he said, gesturing to Endre, "against eighty trained warriors. Well-trained by you if your blood tells us anything. This must be a strategic campaign. It must be well planned, and we must be prepared for an outcome where none of us survive. The situation is not ideal, but the only alternative we have is to allow this degenerate who calls himself The Master to continue to massacre whole villages of humans with the hopes of drawing us out to destroy us. Our only hope is to strike at him first. We will infiltrate from the inside, starting with Endre. Your blood has shown us there are those within the horde who hold a similar mindset as you, they could perhaps even be considered loyal to you. We need you to rally those Vampires to fight the tyrant. But we need you to do it with stealth from the inside. Then, you will cut off the head of the snake and when the time comes to fight, you will have your loyal comrades as well as The Council beside you," Agmundr laid out his plan.

"The Council is an imperative policing body, we cannot afford to fail," Egill added reluctantly. "The tyrant trusts you. He has divulged his plans to you, made you trainer and commander of his troops. We need you to start the battle."

"Do you honestly believe he will welcome me with open arms after having been absent for days?" Endre asked, having already considered the implications of showing up after so long an absence. "They believe I either died or deserted."

"How were you going to carry out your plan before?" Magnhildr pointed out.

"I was going to hope I would not be killed on sight and would be brought before The Master for explanation and could strike him down," Endre said in exasperation.

"And you thought that plan would work?" Egill chuckled.

"I did not expect to walk away. It was the only option I had. Circumstances have changed," Endre countered, giving Egill a scowl.

"What is your plan now?" Agmundr asked.

Endre smiled. He had formulated a new plan, but The Council was not going to like it.

CHAPTER SIXTEEN

Endre led Magnhildr, bound in chains, toward the Vampire horde's camp, trying to keep the smile from his face. He had not thought The Council would consent to his plan, but Magnhildr accepted it without question, agreeing the best way for Endre to curry favor with The Master was for him to bring a member of the entourage. Egill had vehemently rejected the idea when Magnhildr volunteered to be captive.

"Why did you volunteer?" Endre asked as he led her in a wide arc around the encampment so they would approach it from the direction of the village. Part of the plan was to keep the location of the rest of the entourage concealed.

"I have not had the pleasure of meeting The Master, so he will not know who I am when I am presented to him. Both Egill and Agmundr have encountered him on at least one occasion," Magnhildr said, carefully stepping over a fallen log. "He will not know me, so he may not attempt to strike me down immediately. It will also be easier for him to dismiss me as a threat, since I have heard he does not value females as he does males. I may have the opportunity for a private audience."

"But why not send one of the other females? Why come yourself?" Endre inquired, his curiosity genuine.

Magnhildr shook her head slowly before telling him, "I would not put them in harm's way like this. I am the oldest and strongest of our kind, I stand a greater chance of surviving."

That bit of information was news to Endre. He had an inkling The Council was comprised of the most powerful of the Vampires, but he had no idea the female he held in chains before him sat atop that structure.

"If he tastes your blood, he will know who you are," Endre warned, picturing the scene where The Council stood before him, scanning through his memories.

"A benefit of my age is that I have been able to master the will of my blood in many ways. One of those ways being the power to delve deeply into your blood dreams, another is the ability to restrict mine. He will see only what I wish him to see, when I wish him to see it," she explained.

"And you trust me not to kill you before you have a chance to appear before him?" Endre asked.

"You could try," she said with a smirk in her voice, "just as The Master will try. But you would both fail." The confidence in her voice was reassuring to Endre. He had been nervous about taking her instead of one of the males, underestimating her abilities just as she was counting on The Master to do.

"You are the origin of this species, then?" Endre inquired, looking into the distance to judge how far they could go and continue conversing before they needed to play their respective parts of captor and captive. They still had time for her to answer some of his questions.

"No. I do not know our origins. There were legends, once, but they've all since disappeared from oral tradition. I was too young and naïve when I heard them to cherish them as I should have. I am merely the oldest among us, as far as we know. We have rarely ventured from our own lands to seek others across the seas, so it is possible there are others older than I that know where we came from. But what is important is not the past but what we do now to secure a future. I know you have come to loathe this existence in the weeks you have lived it, but I … I have walked as a Vampire for nearly seven centuries," she told him, looking toward the eastern sky where the glow of the sun threatened to break the horizon.

"Seven hundred years," Endre whispered to himself in amazement.

"Yes, and in that time, I have learned there are parts of this life that are undeniably cruel and barbaric. Then again, the same could be said of a human life. But there is also beauty to be found in such longevity," Magnhildr said. "I have traveled all across our land and intend to seek out new terrain to explore once this threat is neutralized. I have learned a great deal, so much more than one could ever hope to learn in a human lifetime. There is always a light in the darkness, Endre. Sometimes you just have to open your eyes wider to see it."

Endre nodded solemnly, letting her words sink in. If she had survived this kind of existence for seven centuries and was not the monster he saw in his own reflection, then perhaps he could do the same.

"We are near the border of the patrol. It is time," Endre warned.

Magnhildr nodded in agreement and began struggling against her bonds, throwing curses into the wind. She allowed him to pull her along behind his horse, making a great show of hurling insults at him and trying to get away. They traveled that way for another few minutes before they crossed the threshold of The Master's territory. His patrols were still a ways off, but Endre knew they would hear the commotion from their posts.

Within moments, a sentry stood before him, and another minute later, he was flanked by two others with weapons drawn.

"Commander?" one of the Vampires asked in surprise, his eyes wide.

"Coward!" one of the others yelled, brandishing his sword in threat.

"We thought you had fallen in the battle," the first Vampire said, his brow creased in confusion.

Endre recognized the first of the Vampires, the one who had spoken as one he would categorize as an ally. The second was decidedly more hostile and fiercely loyal to The Master. The third Vampire, the one who had not spoken, was Gunnar.

"Seems as though he tucked tail and ran," the second Vampire spat.

"Quiet, Berard," Gunnar finally spoke.

"Take his head off where he stands. The Master will commend us for the justice we dealt to this traitor," Berard sneered.

With a roar, Berard lunged to carry out the deed himself. Gunnar placed his body between Berard and Endre's mount and delivered the sentence to Berard he had decreed for Endre with a deft swing of his sword.

The first Vampire who had spoken, whom Endre now remembered was named Ivarr, stood with wide eyes down at Berard's frozen expression of hostility on his severed head. Gunnar barely spared the fallen body a glance before he looked up to Endre atop his horse.

"You should not have come back," Gunnar finally stated.

Endre noted none of the three of them had addressed the bound prisoner he led, who had grown silent behind him. Endre did not know if Magnhildr was afraid or if she merely stood in silent observation. If he had to guess, it would be the latter. He could not envision her fearing anything.

"What of your wife?" Gunnar asked with a deep sigh.

"I thought she would be there, awaiting my return. I was wrong," Endre stated with more emotion than he had allowed himself to exhibit. "I did horrible things and ran from there, too."

"Why did you come back? You were free, why would you come back?" Ivarr asked in puzzlement.

"To stop The Master," Gunnar whispered, his eyes wide.

Endre nodded as understanding passed between him and his friend.

"He cannot be stopped," Ivarr insisted, shaking his head. "There are too many who support him, too many to fight against."

"How many remain after the attack on the village?" Magnhildr asked from beside Endre, catching the attention of Gunnar and Ivarr.

Gunnar eyed Magnhildr curiously before turning to Endre for an explanation.

"She is here to help us," Endre assured his fellow Vampires.

"Who is she?" Gunnar asked suspiciously, making a more thorough appraisal of the female.

"Is he one of yours?" Magnhildr asked Endre, nodding to Gunnar.

"Aye, I am," Gunnar replied.

"What about him?" Magnhildr asked, gesturing with her bound hands to Ivarr.

"Where do you stand, Ivarr?" Endre asked when the other Vampire did not answer for himself like Gunnar had done.

"I am with you, Commander," Ivarr said with a slight bow.

"Good," Magnhildr acknowledged, then turned to Gunnar. "I dare not tell you my name. Though you may not know it, The Master will. I cannot have him know I am in his midst until it is too late. All you need know is I am here of my own will to take part in a scheme to remove The Master from power."

"Kill him, you mean?" Gunnar asked, point blank.

"Indeed," Magnhildr agreed.

"There were fifty-six men remaining after the massacre in the village. You have now replaced Berard as the fifty-sixth," Gunnar told her.

"We lost so many more than I imagined," Endre mused, running his hand over the stubble at his jaw while he pondered how the decrease in numbers affected their odds of winning against the horde.

"How many are steadfast with The Master?" Magnhildr continued her barrage of questions, her tone as commanding as Endre had ever heard it.

"At least twenty. What happened at the village did not sit well with many. Losing the Commander planted some seeds of doubt in their minds about The Master's intentions. Some think The Master knew those villagers were not entirely human and sent us to the slaughter anyway," Ivarr answered, surprising both Gunnar and Endre. "There are at least another dozen or so who may be on the fence. But if you are looking to recruit, I would not announce any plans to those particular Vampires," Ivarr warned.

"Agreed," Gunnar said, nodding vigorously. "I assume you have a plan for all this?"

"We do," Endre said, nodding down to Magnhildr. "She has a contingent of ten warriors on the far side of the camp, just outside hearing range of the patrols. They will join the fray at the next twilight."

"That is not enough time to rally the men who have no allegiance to The Master," Gunnar commented.

Ivarr watched on with a contemplative look before he interjected, "It will have to be. Gunnar and I will speak to them once the sun has risen."

"I will station our men inside the perimeter and station The Master's more loyal Vampires to the outside perimeter," Gunnar said thoughtfully.

Magnhildr nodded. "Our goal is to get me inside the tent with The Master, whether alone or with Endre. We will take down The Master first and work our way outward to the perimeter where the scouts are stationed," she told them.

Gunnar looked to the horizon, where the first rays of sunlight peeked over the bare trees. "Let us get a move on then," he said with a nod. "How are you playing this? Unwilling prisoner? Compliant captive?"

"I think it would be best if I were unconscious when brought before The Master, though do not allow him to taste my blood before I have regained consciousness," Magnhildr cautioned. "I do not think he will believe I would come willingly, and I would like to draw as little attention as possible. We do not want to put the remainder of the horde on edge if we can help it. A small element of surprise will aid us in eliminating The Master and all those loyal to him."

Endre agreed with her assessment, as did Gunnar and Ivarr.

"Are you ready?" Endre asked, dismounting from his horse.

"Yes. It will take me some minutes to revive, so I am putting my life in your hands, Endre. Do not fail me," she whispered, her eyes imploring him not to break her trust.

He did not intend to. In one quick movement, he snapped Magnhildr's neck and caught her body before it hit the ground. Endre hoisted her body up onto his horse and signaled his two allies to lead the way into the camp.

CHAPTER SEVENTEEN

When Endre entered the camp, most of the soldiers were already in their tents, taking their reprieve. But those who caught sight of him being marched between two soldiers gave a range of reactions from hostile to relieved by his presence.

"I hear we have a visitor?" The Master's voice drifted across the camp to where Endre walked.

Endre strode in silence behind Gunnar, leading his horse with an unconscious Magnhildr atop it with Ivarr following behind. None of them acknowledged The Master's comment until they reached his tent.

"Come in, Commander, bring your guest," The Master said, his voice holding a dangerous edge. "You two can go," he said, dismissing Ivarr and Gunnar.

Endre was relieved he had not been clapped in irons immediately. It at least told him The Master still had some trust in him, maybe not much, but enough to keep him agile enough to fight.

"My guards will stay," The Master said with a grin as Endre carried Magnhildr into the tent. "What have we here?" The Master asked, his gaze hungry as it drifted over her body.

He drew closer, his eyes never leaving Magnhildr. His rapt attention made Endre uneasy, but he tried to quell the feeling so The Master did not catch on to it. It would be disastrous to their plans if The Master had an inkling Endre was concerned with what might happen to his prisoner.

"Where ever did you find her?" The Master asked in awe, lightly brushing his fingers down her cheek and moving a lock of hair that was stuck to her eyelashes. The gestures were tender and unlike the cruel and merciless Vampire Endre had come to know.

"She was with her mate. I killed him," Endre stated his rehearsed lines.

"I have never seen a female Vampire before. I have tried to make dozens of them myself, but I have yet to be able to stop myself from taking all when feeding from a woman," The Master said, gazing down at her longingly. "It is a rarity to find a female who can withstand my appetites. I dare say she could do just that," he said before looking up at Endre. "Put her over there," he ordered, waving his hand to the pile of furs which served as his bed.

Endre laid Magnhildr onto the furs, mentally saying a prayer to the gods that The Master had not insisted on a taste to whet that particular appetite. He did not know how he would explain his reluctance to allow The Master to violate her in any way without giving away his true intentions.

"I heard the whispers as you entered the camp that you had returned. At first I thought them ramblings of Vampires who had not abandoned their human superstitions of the spirits of fallen warriors. But here you are, in the flesh. Tell me, Commander, where have you been?" The edge of threat if Endre provided an unsatisfactory answer was unmistakable. If he gave an answer The Master did not like or did not believe, Endre's head would soon be separated from his body.

Endre itched to take The Master now. Give up all pretense of returning to the horde and behead him where he stood. But that would only spell his immediate demise, and likely the failure of the entire campaign. He needed to wait until Magnhildr awoke, and he needed to give Gunnar and Ivarr time to do their parts to ensure everything went along smoothly for them to succeed.

Endre recited to The Master the story Magnhildr, Egill, and Agmundr had concocted. They kept many of the details the same so Endre would not have to lie much. If the entirety of the story was a lie, The Master would catch on quickly to Endre's body's responses to telling the untruths. He told The Master about being in the collapsed building, omitting the part about being attacked by another member of the horde. He then told him he was disoriented when he awoke, not remembering what he was, and made his way home. Endre had not wanted to include the tragic incident with Ingrid in his retelling to The Master, but The Council had insisted it was the strongest blood memory he had right now, so if The Master were to insist on seeing what transpired for himself by partaking in Endre's blood, the murder of Ingrid would be first and foremost of his memories to come forth.

The Council had told Endre The Master was but a few years old, a rogue unwilling to follow the norms of the underground Vampire society. He had ventured to speak to The Council and share his ideas about wanting to make their presence known to the humans and view them solely as the food he believed they were. When Egill and Agmundr heard his ravings, they sentenced him to death, fearing his radical ideas would create unrest amongst the Vampire population, but he escaped.

He had gone to seek out other Vampires who shared his viewpoints to band together as allies. When he could only find proponents for the ways of The Council, he deigned to create his army of followers to destroy those who opposed him. And since he had only spent a few years as a Vampire, he did not possess the same abilities to control blood memories as The Council did, so they did not have any fear of him venturing further into the memories of Endre's blood to see the meeting or planning that had taken place between them.

The Master grinned at him gleefully when he recounted how he had found his wife in bed with another man and killed them both. Clearly, he did not hear the undercurrent of distress in Endre's voice; he only envisioned the thirst for revenge he imagined there.

"And here you are," The Master said triumphantly. "A good kill will always bring you back to your senses," he said sagely.

"I came upon her and her mate on my journey back here," Endre explained, drawing The Master's attention once again back to Magnhildr.

"And you thought to bring her to me as a gift," The Master said with a chuckle. "Well done. She is the rarest gift I have ever received. She's certainly the loveliest."

As if hearing The Master calling her lovely was her cue, Magnhildr's eyes fluttered open. Endre was unsure if it was part of her ruse, or if even the act of waking was done with the same grace with which she performed every other movement. Endre had only woken with a jolt since his transformation. There had been no lazy lifting of the eyelids—only panic. He supposed it could have been her seven hundred years of practice dealing with blood dreams which allowed her such a smooth transition into the waking world.

"So lovely," The Master whispered with that depraved smile that made Endre's skin crawl.

CHAPTER EIGHTEEN

Magnhildr sat up and met The Master's gaze with a fierce one of her own. She appeared as a Valkyrie personified, her fiery hair a halo that caught the morning sun's muted rays as they shone through the fabric of the tent. Endre worried her obvious disdain would ruin the ploy. They needed The Master to view her as weak and pliable.

The Master grasped Magnhildr's hair and yanked her to her feet. The sudden change from the tender way he had stroked her cheek to the violent about-face was surprising to Endre. He took a step forward, unsure if he should intervene or wait to see how things played out. While The Master was occupied with what he thought was his new plaything, Endre made a subtle search of the tent, cataloging the locations of any weapons.

"What were you doing so near my encampment?" The Master asked Magnhildr in a rough voice. "Have you been sent by The Council to challenge me?"

"N-no," Magnhildr stuttered, "my mate and I were just passing through."

Endre had to admit she was doing a superb job. If he did not know what she was really like, he would have believed she was meek and frightened of The Master. This was all part of the plan—get him to believe she was easily overpowered so he did not view her as a threat. They hoped it would get his guard down and allow them to make their move without much anticipation on his part. They just had to wait until The Master thought her docile enough to turn his back and for their allies to do their parts and get into position.

"We shall see if you speak the truth," The Master said, turning back to look at Endre, Magnhildr's hair still gripped in his fist. "Both of you."

Endre held out his wrist, exposing the flesh between his hand and his shirt cuff, enticing The Master to have a taste. He did not disappoint. Without preamble, The Master gripped Endre's arm with his free hand and sank his fangs into Endre's wrist. Endre struggled to not make any sounds of pain that may be perceived as weakness, but The Master was making a point to not be gentle.

Endre tried to clear his mind and envision his tragic reunion with Ingrid—just as Magnhildr taught him—in an attempt to deter The Master from viewing any of the memories of his blood that had occurred afterward. After a few great draws, The Master detached from Endre's wrist and shoved him away with a growl. Blood dripped from his chin and traveled its way down his neck, where it pooled in the furs of his cloak.

Then, The Master turned his attention to where Magnhildr sat still as a statue, waiting for her turn. She offered up her bound wrists. The corners of The Master's mouth turned up in a devilish smile, and before Endre could move to stop him, The Master pulled Magnhildr toward him by the hair and sank his fangs into her throat with the fierce brutality of a predator intent on taking the life of its prey. She cried out in pain, the sound gut-wrenching to Endre's ears. Endre moved to pull The Master from Magnhildr, but she opened her eyes so they met Endre's. He expected her to plead for his help with her gaze, but it told him only to hold steady. Wait and see, her eyes told him.

After several agonizing minutes, which felt to Endre more like years, The Master pulled his fangs from Magnhildr's neck with a sigh of contentment. Where his face had looked gruesome after feeding from Endre's wrist, now The Master's entire jaw, neck, and the front of his shirt were stained crimson. He looked to Endre like a great beast gorging himself on the raw meat of his prey's carcass.

Magnhildr's wound closed quickly, just as Endre's had at his wrist, but the blood that had escaped from The Master's greedy drafts slicked down the side of her neck, drenching the front of her dress. The Master stumbled backward toward a chair and sank into it, his head thrown back and his eyes closed.

Endre stood still, watching the other Vampire for any sign he may have seen some incriminating memory, but other than the rapid movement of his eyes beneath the lids and the shallow rise and fall of his chest with his breaths, The Master did not move. Endre looked to Magnhildr for guidance on their next move, but her eyes were still watching The Master. Endre's sight landed on a sheathed sword across the tent, his mind reasoning with him that now was the most opportune time to take The Master's head. They would likely not get a chance where he would be so vulnerable again.

As if sensing the danger he was in, The Master woke from his sudden slumber, his eyes burning into Endre, who snapped his gaze from the weapon to The Master's face at the first sign of his waking. His eyes slid slowly over to Magnhildr, and Endre wondered what it was he had seen in the memories she had put into her blood.

"The ability to see into the memories of another's blood is truly a great gift. For many it takes years, even centuries, to develop the control over the blood to show and see what one wills. For others, such as myself, the ability to harness that level of control is developed at a much quicker rate. Did you know, Commander, that consuming the blood of other Vampires accelerates the aging process?" The Master said without taking his eyes from Magnhildr.

The fine hairs on the back of Endre's neck raised in alarm. Magnhildr had mentioned The Master had learned many secrets in his short time as a Vampire, but this one she had not mentioned. "Did you think I would not sense your power in your blood?" The Master whispered to Magnhildr. "High Councilor," he added with a hiss.

In a flash of movement, Endre dove for the sword he had been eying earlier, and Magnhildr broke the weak chains Endre had used to bind her. She had no more removed the links before The Master was upon her.

Endre managed to unsheathe his borrowed sword just as The Master pulled one Endre had not realized was strapped at his waist from its scabbard. The blade pressed into Magnhildr's throat, already cutting into her flesh, but The Master held back from taking her head.

"What an honor to have the High Councilor herself come to take my life. It is truly my life's greatest moment being in your presence," The Master sneered into her ear.

Endre leveled his sword to The Master's neck and he chuckled.

"I will have her head clean off before you can so much as swing," The Master taunted him.

"I care not what happens to her, as I will send you to Hel," Endre told him, the coldness in his voice real. He truly did not want Magnhildr to die, but there were always casualties in war. In this instance, he considered it the sacrifice of one for the good of the many. If The Master were allowed to live, many more would suffer.

"Ever the idealistic, ruthless, warrior, hmmm, Endre?" The Master said, wiggling the blade he had lodged into Magnhildr's neck back and forth, creating a fresh cascade of blood.

With a roar, Endre drew back his sword and aimed for the spot where The Master's head met his shoulder. The unexpected clash of metal meeting metal assaulted Endre's ears, as did the dull thud of Magnhildr's body falling to the ground. The Master warded off Endre's second blow when the first failed with a change in position of his blade. Endre's focus was solely on The

Master and his deadly steel, his concern for Magnhildr's fallen body forgotten.

Endre and The Master traded blows, testing the strength of the other. Endre had shown his skill with a blade on the training field with the other Vampires, so The Master knew what he was capable of, but Endre had never seen The Master wield a weapon. As steel met steel, Endre came to realize The Master was stronger than him but less skilled with a blade. Endre sought to use this to his advantage by employing unpredictable maneuvers he had not displayed on the training field. He had shown the other Vampires of the horde the basic moves needed to defend and attack, but he had not displayed his full skill-set, and he needed that element of surprise if he had any hope of beating The Master.

Sounds from outside the tent caught Endre's attention. It seemed they were going to have to put their plan into place earlier than first anticipated. Even through the material of the tent, Endre could see it was still some time before dusk. The sound of all-out war broke out outside the thin barrier the tent provided, and The Council's reinforcements were not due to intervene until the sun set. Whoever Ivarr and Gunnar had managed to recruit to their cause were left on their own to fight The

Master and any warriors still loyal to him. The scenario spelled certain doom.

Endre tried not to let the thoughts of his friends and their collective imminent demise distract him from his bout with The Master. In the end, it was the fall of The Master which mattered most. When Endre had endeavored to take The Master's life, he thought him merely a lunatic with a complete lack of morals and compassion, but now he knew he held power that rivaled the High Councilor, who likely lay dead at his feet. The Master could not be allowed to continue building his army and destroying everything that lay in his path.

While his back was to it, the flap of the tent flew open, and Endre felt the presence of several Vampires. He forced himself not to pull his attention from The Master, who lunged at him, to gauge if these newcomers were a threat, but Endre knew they were.

"Do not interfere. I will dispatch this ungrateful miscreant myself!" The Master ordered the Vampires who had entered the tent to come to his aid.

Endre pressed on, fighting with everything he was worth. He knew even if he took The Master apart piece by piece like he longed to, he would not live long after. His guards and his staunch supporters who guarded the entrance to the tent would make sure of that. Sweat built up on Endre's brow from the effort of the fight, a sensation he had yet to experience as a Vampire. In training, the effort expended had been only a fraction of what he endured now. He could feel himself tiring, and was actually surprised to find he did not have an unlimited well of strength to pull from. The thought was disheartening, considering The Master showed no such signs of weakness. Endre was going to fail.

"You will lose," The Master taunted. "I can already see you tiring."

Endre said nothing. There was no use in denying the plain truth in front of him. The Master was right, his body was weakening, his resolve right along with it. The thought of failure rang in Endre's ears, the self-doubt permeating his brain like a poison. His moves became sloppy as his body grew more exhausted, and he took more than a few blows from The Master's blade. When The Master's blade sliced across his calf, Endre let out a roar of pain and fell to his knees. This was it. His second end.

The Master wore a sick, gloating smile as he took Endre down to his knees. Seeing the depravity in his smile snapped something inside Endre. He would not allow this monster to get the better of him. Never again. Endre's vision blurred with red at the edges, and he felt the berserker within struggling to break free. Endre tossed open the doors with which he kept the animal caged and allowed it to take him over. He had fought valiantly to keep the monster within locked up, but he now realized he needed his monster to defeat a monster.

Endre's movements were a blur of limbs and steel as he snatched up his blade where it had fallen and rose to his feet in one quick movement. The Master's expression turned to one of surprise, but only for a moment, before it disappeared and was replaced by white-hot rage.

"You will not walk out of here," Endre informed The Master through gritted teeth. His words erupted with such conviction even he believed them.

With one swing of his blade, Endre ended The Master's second life, the surprised expression frozen on his now-severed head.

CHAPTER NINETEEN

Endre stood over The Master's fallen body. His chest heaved with his labored breaths, and his head was filled with the rushing sound of his blood pounding adrenaline through his limbs. He had succeeded. He had killed The Master. Though he had yet to conquer his inner demons, he had been able to dispatch his tormentor made of flesh and blood.

"It is not over yet," Magnhildr announced, drawing Endre's surprised gaze to where she sat on the ground. He had thought The Master's blade to the neck had claimed her life. She nodded to something behind him, and it was at that moment he was reminded of the Vampire guards who had witnessed The Master's death sentence carried out.

Heaving in one last breath, Endre swung to face the guards. He had expected to be met with Vampires with swords drawn, ready to run him through for his treachery. The guards stood staring at him in awe, seemingly unable to decipher what they were to do now.

"Do you surrender?" Endre asked them, unsure how to handle this particular scenario. Did they intend to fight him? To join him?

"Ivarr sent us here to assist you," one Vampire spoke quietly.

Endre let out a relieved breath. His energy was sapped, and he knew there was no way he would have been able to take on the lot of them in his exhausted state.

"You need to help the others," Magnhildr ordered, drawing everyone's attention to the sounds of sword strikes and death outside the confines of the tent.

The soldiers before them nodded in agreement and hurried from the tent to engage in the fray. Endre moved to follow them but was stopped by Magnhildr's hand grasping his arm.

"You are too weak to fight," she admonished. "If you go out there, you will surely die."

Endre looked down at her fingers gripping him desperately. He did not know why she would care if he lived or died. She had wanted to use him as bait from the beginning, so her sudden interest in his welfare was surprising. But he was a warrior; he could not send his brethren into a battle that spelled out certain doom and cower behind a tent. That was not the way to redeem his place in Valhalla.

"I cannot send them to the slaughter," Endre insisted, trying to pull his arm from her grasp.

"Instead you would follow them into it?" Magnhildr scowled darkly. "What does anyone gain by your death?"

"What does anyone gain by my life? My mission here was always to send The Master to his second death," Endre started.

"And you have done your part," Magnhildr interrupted.

"Now, there are others out there just like him," Endre shouted, pointing his sword in the direction of the fighting outside the tent, "killing my friends while I stand and argue with you."

"I would keep you safe here, you lack the strength to prevent me," she warned.

"What do you gain from keeping me safe?" Endre asked, eyeing her suspiciously.

"You have saved my life, I only wish to save yours," she told him humbly.

Endre continued his assessment of her. He did not believe her. She was not attempting to keep him from the fight to spare him the pain of a second death; she had to have some ulterior motive. She had already sought to manipulate him once for her own gain; he did not see how the same would not be true of her now.

"Lies," Endre hissed, yanking on his arm, but her grip only tightened.

"The Council needs you," she blurted out, her eyes taking on the sheen of desperation Endre had yet to see in her.

"What could I possibly have that The Council requires?" Endre scoffed.

"You are a great warrior. You have a mind for strategy and planning. We are in need of your skills. What I offer to you is a great honor. Come with me now, leave the horde to destroy itself," she demanded.

Endre had the High Councilor begging for him to join her entourage. He was sure other Vampires would clamor for the honor. He saw no honor in leaving his comrades to fight a battle he had started.

"I will not run from a fight. You and yours gave your word you would help destroy The Master's horde, and yet now you ask me to flee with you? To run like a coward and turn my back on my fellow warriors? There is no honor in your request," Endre seethed. He ripped his arm from her grasp and stormed from the tent. He would not send his men into certain doom alone.

CHAPTER TWENTY

The bright sunlight blinded Endre as he emerged from the tent. He had almost forgotten dusk had not yet fallen. A pair of Vampires fought in front of him, and he used his blade to make quick work of his enemy before moving through the camp looking for more of The Master's loyal followers to send along the same path to Hel. The ground between tents was littered with bodies belonging to both his allies and his enemies. The fight had ended. In the time Magnhildr had kept him captive in the tent with her argument, The Master's horde had been decimated, along with a fair number of his allies.

Endre turned in a slow circle, taking in the death all around him. Where were the victors? He raced through the camp, searching inside and between each tent for survivors. He came up empty-handed until he reached the clearing that served as the training field. In it, he saw several Vampires dragging the bodies of the fallen across the matted grass to a massive pile. He watched with his mouth agape as each new body drawn to the pile was systematically beheaded before being added.

With each body of his friends added, a pang went through his chest. If he had been out here fighting, he could have saved them.

"You would have died if you were out here," Magnhildr's voice came from behind him.

Endre whirled around, pointing his sword at her heart. "At least it would have been honorable," he retorted.

"There is no honor in dying needlessly. The gods need you less for their war than we need you here," she told him, holding her hands out in surrender. She appealed to his sense of honor, knowing he would not strike her down while unarmed. He longed for her to produce a blade from her skirts so he had an excuse to run her through. "It is over now. Sheath your sword and come with me."

Endre shook his head. "My place is not with The Council."

"Then where is it you imagine you belong?" she asked, her eyebrows raised in question. "The only place you do belong is with The Council. The human world is no place for Vampires, you cannot go back to it," she warned.

"I plan to make my own place," he remarked before lowering his sword and turning his back to her. He knew it was unwise to scorn her offer, but he would not be able to live with himself if he accepted. Once again, he was arguing with the High Councilor when his men needed him.

Endre strode toward the pile of bodies, catching sight of Gunnar at the edge. The other Vampire severed a head from the body of one of The Master's guards and tossed both parts up onto the pile that rose well over his head.

"Commander," Gunnar greeted him when he approached.

"Gunnar," Endre said, looking around at the handful of Vampires around them. Three. He counted three of them, none of which were the Vampire with which he wished to speak. "Where is Ivarr?"

Gunnar hung his head, his features twisted with pain. "Fallen, Sir. Right after you ended The Master."

Endre hung his head along with Gunnar in a silent prayer for their fallen comrade. His chest constricted with the pain of the loss. He had known all along there was a high probability of losing his allies, just as he expected to lose his own life, but he did not expect to still be standing while Ivarr had met his end. He had assumed they would both live or die together in this fight.

When the last body had been added to the pile, Endre nodded to Gunnar to light the pyre. He watched with the other three Vampires as the flames devoured friend and foe alike. The scent of seared flesh infiltrated his nostrils, but he refused to turn away. These warriors gave their lives in battle, and he would not dishonor them by turning his back on them.

"You did not go with The Council," Gunnar said to him, a statement rather than a question. Endre swore he heard a note of admonishment in his tone.

"No, I did not. But neither did you," he replied. The Council had offered a place to each of the other three warriors who had survived the battle. The two besides Gunnar had accepted the honor to serve as bodyguards, but Gunnar turned them down, just as Endre had.

"Why?" Gunnar asked, his curiosity clearing him of any inclination he might have had against questioning the Vampire who had once been his superior.

"I did not agree with them," Endre said with a shrug.

"With what exactly?" Gunnar inquired.

"Who they protect. They seek to protect only the Vampires, not humans," Endre said with disgust. When Gunnar did not reply and instead gave him a confused look, Endre continued, "Vampires are not the ones who need protecting from the humans. Maybe from Hunters, but humans are the ones who need protection from the likes of us."

Gunnar nodded and turned back to the blaze burning before them. Endre knew he felt it, too—the monster within. If he did not, he would not have been fighting on the same side as Endre and would instead be a corpse on the pile before them.

"Where will you go now?" Gunnar asked, still facing the fire.

"I have always longed to cross the sea. I think I will start there," Endre said with a shrug. He had not had the time to formulate the details of his new plan yet, but he knew the general direction he was headed.

"What will you do there? Protect humans?" the other Vampire asked skeptically.

"I intend to," Endre said, turning to face Gunnar's profile. "From Vampires like The Master. From themselves."

Gunnar shook his head. "We have been a part of both worlds. How can you protect them from themselves?" he asked with a chuckle.

"I intend to prey on the worst of them. The ones who seek to make victims of their brothers," Endre said with a devilish smile. His desire to roam the human world by cover of darkness, hunting down the dregs of society, burned within him. He saw it as his penance, the way he could atone for the monster inside. "Where will you go? What will you do?"

"I do not know," Gunnar said. "Maybe I will follow you across the sea," he said with a grin.

Endre clapped him on the shoulder with his big hand. "Then so you shall," he said with a smile of his own.

The pair gathered their arms and turned their backs on the mountain of flames that reached high to kiss the night sky. It would be a long walk to the sea. But a new life free of servitude to any master awaited them across those waters and was well worth the journey.

TARA VASSER

IRRESISTIBLE
2ND EDITION

BOOK ONE

THE BLOODLUST CHRONICLES

TARA VASSER

IRRESISTIBLE

Buried as punishment for a crime he didn't commit, Endre has had nothing but time to plot revenge on his betrayer. Salvation arrives when an archaeology student unwittingly exhumes his coffin and provides him with the first blood he's tasted in nearly a century.

Upon awakening from an attack by a creature she never believed existed, Nora discovers she is now his hostage. Forced to accompany Endre from Italy to Paris on a quest for vengeance, she is thrust into his dark and forbidden world and finds herself inexplicably drawn to the Vampire. Lust runs rampant throughout the course of their journey and Nora begins to question if the irresistible connection between them is more than mere biology.

PROLOGUE
1923-Italy

Endre sat beneath the shadow of a massive cork tree in his garden, reading the newspaper as he watched the first rays of sunshine peek over the hills to the east. It was a pity he could not give his full attention to the beautiful view, his mind burdened with the troubling headlines. Folding the paper with a deep sigh, he pushed the paper and his thoughts of Mussolini's latest moves to overtake parliament to the side. Perhaps it was time to leave Italy and move on to greener pastures. There was an ominous scent in the wind, and it spoke of the death and destruction on the horizon.

Endre was no stranger to war and chaos, having been born a warrior. When conflicts arose in the world around him, his hands always itched to take up sword and shield. But of course, those days of ending wars with steel were over. Now, the weapons of choice were guns and bombs. There was no honor in that. No promises of glory or feasting in the halls of Valhalla when so little skill and preparation was involved.

Valhalla or no, the political climate of this region was no longer hospitable to his research. Secrecy was completely necessary, and the alliances Gregor had forged to provide Endre with supplies for his lab would not stand the threat this new breed of fascism posed. Glancing over at the horizon, he frowned. He had been out here long enough; it was time to retire for the day, and he would allow his dreams to conjure his next moves and put new plans into place when twilight fell. Endre picked up his paper and made his way toward the door when the noise of automobile tires crunching over the gravel drive and shouting stilled his movement.

"Back here! In the garden!" a voice hollered from the garden entrance.

A man dressed impeccably in a suit with a homburg gracing his head stood at the entrance of the sanctuary. Endre did not recall his name, he only knew the man as one of Lorenzo's bodyguards. The man gestured wildly in Endre's direction.

Several more of Lorenzo's bodyguards filed in behind him, posturing menacingly.

Confused, Endre watched the men as they lined the perimeter of his garden, violating his last few moments before the sun crested over the hill. "What is this? Where is Lorenzo?" he scoffed, standing his ground when they surrounded him where he stood, preparing to fight if the need arose.

"I am here," Lorenzo's French-accented voice called leisurely from the garden entrance as he strolled forward and casually buttoned his suit jacket.

Sighing with relief, Endre relaxed at the sight of his friend.

Lorenzo sauntered into the garden lazily, stopping to inspect a blossom before meandering his way through his men to stand in front of Endre.

"And to what do I owe this honor?" Endre questioned suspiciously, watching Lorenzo carefully. It was much too close to dawn for them to be conducting business.

"Endre, you have been charged with murder," Lorenzo recited in a bored voice, placing his hands in his pockets and rocking back on his heels.

Endre's head jerked back as if he had been struck. Murder? He was being charged with murder? "And who is it exactly that I am supposed to have killed?" Endre demanded, outrage making his voice boom through the still morning air.

"Count La Rossa." Lorenzo sighed sadly. "Why did you do it, Endre?"

"You cannot be serious." Endre balked, sure this was some prank. "Gregor is dead?"

The men surrounding him took a step closer, as if of one mind.

"I did not kill Gregor," Endre protested, though he found himself falling back on his training from another life and crouched into a fighting stance.

Several more men joined the mob, men from Gregor's guard, flanking Endre now with more than a dozen men. At most, he could take out half of them before they would bring him down, leaving another half dozen to beat him mercilessly and likely kill him in the process—merely for resisting. Any defiance would be futile, but he would not go down without a fight, especially for a false charge.

Lorenzo shook his head sadly at Endre's change in demeanor, as if his instincts of self-preservation condemned him of the crimes for which he was accused. Lorenzo raised his voice loud so all the men could hear him. "Endre, you are hereby charged with the murder of Count Gregor La Rossa. Your brothers here will serve as judge, jury, and executioners of your sentence. The traditional punishment for such a crime, as you are well aware, is burial. Your death by starvation will serve as justice by the old laws laid forth by The Council. Guards, seize him and prepare him for his punishment." Then, turning back to Endre, he taunted, "I think we will bury you here in your beloved garden."

Several of the guards pulled out pistols and made moves toward Endre.

Cowards, of course, they would not face him without firearms.

Endre lashed out, but he had only his fists. He managed to knock two of the guards to the ground before they had him pinned to the moldering leaves in the dirt.

Fists were no match for bullets.

Watching with one eye—the other caked in blood and dirt—three men began digging his grave beneath the large tree and another two hauled a plain coffin through the garden gates.

At the sight of the coffin, Endre redoubled his struggled to break free. "Lorenzo, this is nonsense. Gregor was my oldest friend and confidant. He was like a brother to me, just as you are. I would never harm him. What is the evidence against me? I demand a trial with The Council. It is my right," he spoke around the dirt in his mouth.

Scowling down at him disapprovingly, Lorenzo approached slowly. He stooped and picked up Endre's fallen fedora, brushing dirt from the fabric.

An entreating glance at Lorenzo earned Endre naught but a kick to the face. This man was no friend. Endre wondered if he had ever been. Blood from a gash above his eye poured down his face, but healed almost as quickly as it occurred, leaving dried blood caked to his eyelashes.

Through crusted lashes, he watched as Lorenzo stood above him and removed his own hat, placing Endre's atop his head instead.

Smiling, Lorenzo gave a nod of approval at Endre's taste in men's fashion and tossed his hat to one of the men standing guard, inciting a round of chuckles from his henchmen.

Fury boiled in Endre's veins as his 'friend' betrayed him and made light of the unlawful punishment he dealt. How could Lorenzo believe Endre capable of such a crime? It was unlike Lorenzo to dole out consequence without following proper protocol.

Unless Lorenzo had something to hide. Something he worried The Council would unearth if the matter were brought to trial.

Realization sunk like a stone in Endre's gut as he put the pieces together.

When the guards finished digging the grave, the men casually tossed the coffin into the pit at Lorenzo's gesture. The dull thud sent a chill through Endre. He continued to struggle against his captors, but with three of them now detaining him, he received nothing but a pistol whip to the head and kicks to his ribs.

With a nod from Lorenzo, the guards hauled Endre to his feet and dragged him toward the yawning opening of the coffin awaiting him. At the foot of the open box, two of the guards held his arms while one bound his hands in front of him with thick rope. Endre let out a shout when one man grabbed his hair and held his head back so he gazed directly into the lightening sky. From the corner of his eye, Endre watched Lorenzo pull a wicked-looking dagger from a sheath at his hip. The blade glinted with the light of the rising sun, a shining omen of Endre's imminent demise.

"Lorenzo, please," Endre spoke to the man before him, the man he had considered a friend until this day, "I—"

Lorenzo only gave Endre a devious grin and prevented any more words from escaping his lips with a quick slash of his blade across Endre's neck. Blood cascaded from his neck and he choked as it drained into his throat. Within seconds, the wound had already begun to heal itself, the blood flow stanched. Lorenzo's blade dashed out again, performing the same motion across the nearly-healed laceration. Again, Endre choked and sputtered on his own warm blood and any words he wished to speak.

Light-headed from the blood loss, Endre fell to his knees. The guards holding him stepped back and left him with Lorenzo glowering down at him. Endre's head lolled to the side and he was barely clinging to consciousness. All it took was a well-placed kick from Lorenzo and he fell backward into his new prison.

Several of the guards made a move to place the lid on the coffin, but Lorenzo stayed their movement with a wave of his hand. "Leave us. I want to speak to this murderous traitor alone before we leave him to the worms," Lorenzo ordered, his eyes never leaving Endre's fading ones.

Several murmurs went through the small crowd. That was not the way. Tradition and adherence to the old laws stated the sentence must be carried out before an amassing of the people, so all could witness what fate befell a murderer of his own kind.

"Leave us!" Lorenzo roared, turning to stare down each man in turn.

The guards filed from the garden, leaving Endre with Lorenzo and his bloody blade.

Lorenzo couched so his face was close to Endre's.

Endre only wished enough blood had still flowed in his veins so he could reach out and relieve Lorenzo of the triumphant smile gracing his lips.

"Endre," Lorenzo whispered with a sigh, "I warned you not to approach Gregor to back your research, and yet you did. Not only that, expressing wishes to distribute your cure at no cost?" Lorenzo tsked and shook his head. "He would have done it, too. Threatened to expose me for lack of loyalty to our people. Unfortunately, he miscalculated. The man was too much of a philanthropist for his own good. He never did understand the power his money held. Such a waste. And here we are. Someone has to take the fall for Gregor's death and *justice* must be served. It might as well be you. His blood is on your hands as much as mine, all because you could not follow simple directions.

We could have profited from this together, you and I. I would kill you now if it would not upset the delicate sensibilities of our people. But alas, I cannot. Perhaps in a century or two, I will come check on you and finish the task when everyone has forgotten your existence."

Endre glared up at Lorenzo, the lack of blood preventing his wounds from healing and allowing him to foil his new enemy's plans.

"But do not worry," Lorenzo continued, brushing dirt from his trousers. "I will not let your research go to waste. I still have plans for the work you have done, but perhaps an adjustment here and there to suit my own needs."

Endre only had the faintest inkling of what kind of dastardly plans Lorenzo was concocting, but the malicious smile gracing his lips was indication enough that it would not be good.

Rising to his feet, Lorenzo glanced down impassively at Endre once more. "You should have listened to me, old friend. Now, you will have plenty of time to think on your cure and the error of your ways while you rot in your grave," Lorenzo spat out with a maniacal laugh. Bending over, he slashed out with his blade one last time.

Endre felt the slightest trickle of blood ooze from the cut, so little of the liquid remained in his body.

At a shouted order from Lorenzo, the guards all marched back into the garden.

Endre attempted to alert them to Lorenzo's treachery, but the only sound from his mangled throat was a pained moan. The lid of the coffin was lowered, blocking out the dazzling sunshine of the new morning, and hammers pounded out the finality of his death sentence. The last glimpse Endre had of Lorenzo was a mocking tip of the hat, *his* hat.

This box would not hold Endre forever, and when he rose, he intended to rain down retribution, and when he came for Lorenzo, it would be all-out war. The last thing he could hear between his own thoughts of revenge and each shovelful of dirt falling on the wooden box was Lorenzo whistling happily with the belief he had gotten away with his crimes.

CHAPTER ONE

"Alright, class, that's it for today's lecture," Professor Hoffman concluded before turning back to face his students. "However," he shouted above the suddenly deafening noise of books shoved into backpacks and students rushing to get to their next classes, "I do have a few announcements."

The entire class groaned in unison and the din died down to a rustle of papers and the occasional zipper.

Nora's attention snapped from the bluebird hopping from branch to branch in the enormous oak tree outside the lecture hall's window to Professor Hoffman at the front of the room. It wasn't like her to allow her thoughts to drift so much during class. In fact, she usually loved this course. Lately, though, she was finding it difficult to concentrate through the haze of exhaustion. Even her roommate Chloe had noticed her dragging, forcing Nora to make an appointment with the campus clinic.

"There is a dig opportunity in Italy that has just come up," the professor hinted, pausing for the class's rapt attention, which he quickly received.

It was as if a switch had been flicked and all the air was sucked from the room. The silence was stifling. Every student held their breath, waiting for the rest of the announcement. Even Nora's attention was single-mindedly focused on the professor.

Most days, she just wanted to blend into the crowd, avoiding eye contact, lest she get called on to answer questions. She didn't like being singled out in class discussions to point out that she knew the answers. She'd told herself during her senior year of high school that college would change her label as nerd or a geek. She would have adventures, friends and fun. Nora had planned to dress up in sexy little dresses and attend wild parties where she would drink too much and dance with wild abandon. But here she was still the responsible, studious one, four years later. This announcement could make the lack of fun and wild abandon all worthwhile; it could be just what she needed to make that hard work pay off and jumpstart a career for when she graduated.

"Since this is a prime opportunity for a select few of you to gain some field experience, I am restricting the applications to seniors only," the professor said, his voice booming through the lecture hall amidst the groans of the underclassmen, whose attention evaporated into the ether. "If you are a senior, and you have a B plus or above, I welcome your applications. I have them up here," he enticed, thumbing the edge of the papers as though he was counting a small fortune. "Come to the front of the room with questions. Class is dismissed."

Her exhaustion all but absent, Nora rushed to the front of the room. The dig was a once in a lifetime opportunity she *had* to know more about.

"Nora!" Professor Hoffman exclaimed with a smile as she approached his desk. "Are you applying for the dig?"

"I was still debating, actually," Nora wavered, biting her lip and forcing her gaze upward from her shoes to meet his eyes.

"There's nothing to debate. You've got the top grade in the class. I will guarantee one of the three spots is yours if you want to go," he affirmed, leaning back against the desk and crossing his arms, an expression akin to disapproval settling on his face.

Nora's eyes grew wide as her brain attempted to process what he had just said. He was *guaranteeing* her a spot? Disbelief and a little bit of terror stole all other thoughts from her brain.

"Think about it, but not too long," he warned, handing Nora a sheet of paper before returning to the other side of the desk to retrieve his laptop bag.

Nora hardly noticed him leave as she stared at the paper gripped in her shaking hands. Dropping her backpack to the floor, she sank into the seat of the nearest desk, worried her shaking legs would fail her.

This was it. This was her big adventure.

Fate had brought this opportunity to her; it would be bad manners to fling it back in her face, wouldn't it? Quickly pulling a pen from her backpack, Nora filled out the form, trying to ignore the tremors making her writing nearly illegible. Once every space was filled in, she threw her pen back into her bag and pulled her bag onto her back with renewed vigor. Running down the hall to Professor Hoffman's office, she was determined to put the form into his hands before she lost her nerve, barely catching him before he locked his door.

"Here," she panted, thrusting the paper at him. "I'm in. I want to go," she announced, pushing her glasses up the bridge of her nose.

Professor Hoffman broke into a huge grin. He took the paper from her and shook her sweaty, shaking hand. "Welcome aboard, Nora!" he exclaimed excitedly. "Come here on Wednesday around noon for a meeting to go through the particulars."

Nora nodded mutely as Professor Hoffman brushed past her and left her standing in the hall outside his office, paralyzed with disbelief. She was going to Italy on her first real archeological dig. Suppressing an uncharacteristic excited squeal which threatened to escape from her, she sprinted the whole way back to her dorm, thoughts of exhaustion and blood tests completely forgotten.

In less than two weeks, Nora would be in a different country on a different continent. It was all exciting, overwhelming, and absolutely terrifying.

CHAPTER TWO

Over the next several days leading up to departure for the trip, Nora alternately attempted to pack everything she could possibly need for an international trip and tried desperately not to throw up. In her head, she made big plans to travel across Italy and see the sights in Rome, Florence, Venice, and wherever her dreams took her. Lying on her stomach with her feet kicked up in the air like a teenage girl looking through a gossip magazine, she pored over the Italy travel guide she'd picked up from the campus bookstore.

"Firenze. Venezia," Nora whispered to herself, trying out the foreign words on her tongue. Memorizing every detail of the pictures and attempting to wrap her brain around the Italian pronunciations, she worked on narrowing down her wish list of tourist traps.

"Are you still reading that thing?" Chloe, her best friend and roommate, inquired with a laugh. "Are you actually going to see all those places you've marked with your little tabs?" She gestured to the fluorescent pink slips of paper protruding from the guidebook.

"I want to! I just don't know if I'll be able to." Nora groaned, burying her face in her pillow.

"Why not?" Chloe pressed, sitting next to her on the bed and taking the book. Flipping through the pages, she stopped to admire several pictures of the Ponte Vecchio in Florence Nora had tagged. "Will you be working the entire time, or do you get weekends off to go see these things?" she asked, waving the book at her roommate.

"It's not time I'm worried about. I just don't know if I can do it, you know?" Nora whined, rolling onto her side and reaching for the book.

"No, I don't know, Nora," Chloe countered, narrowing her eyes and holding the book out of Nora's grasp. "You get this incredible opportunity to travel to Italy. Freaking *Italy*, Nora. You damn well better go and see all this stuff, this is all you've ever wanted to do with your life. I know it's not Norway, or whatever your dream destination is, but Italy has some amazing rich history and mythology."

It was true. She'd always known she wanted to study lives and stories of the past. The influence of her grandmother's elaborate tales of Norse mythology were to blame for Nora's single-minded determination to study archaeology.

Nodding, Nora reached for the book again. "We're going to this estate in Tuscany, just outside of Siena. It's owned by a guy Professor Hoffman knows, Mr. Micelli. I guess he's refurbishing this big villa to make it into a fancy spa. The construction crew was digging to repair the foundation and they found something he thinks might be an ancient Roman artifact."

"Why fly people all the way from the U.S. instead of using students from Italy?" Chloe questioned, frowning at a page in the book.

"I don't know, I suppose because he knows and trusts Professor Hoffman? Really, I'm not sure. Something about checking into it before the government seizes it." Nora shrugged. All the information came at her so fast when the professor was explaining everything to her and the other two attending students, she hadn't really had much time to absorb it all.

"That sounds fishy. I mean, it's probably on the up and up, but it's kind of weird," Chloe said as she furrowed her brow when meeting Nora's gaze.

"I don't think Professor Hoffman would get us into something illegal. At least not intentionally," Nora defended. She'd had Professor Hoffman for a few different classes now, and he did not strike her as the type to get involved with illegal activities. Nora reached for the book again, worried all Chloe's paging would dislodge her carefully placed tags.

"Who else is going?" Chloe held the book away from Nora's grabbing hands while she flipped to each bright pink page marker.

"Two other people from my class, Tom and Judy, I think their names are." Nora wracked her brain for confirmation on the names. She wasn't the most social of people, preferring books to human interaction most times, so the names of her classmates didn't usually stick with her.

"Is he cute?"

"Who?"

"Professor Hoffman," Chloe said with a guffaw, then rolled her eyes. "The Tom guy from your class."

"I don't know, kinda, I guess so."

"What about the Italian guy?" Chloe peeked up over the edge of the book with a smirk.

"I haven't seen him, so I don't know." Nora shrugged.

"But he's Italian, and has enough money to buy property in Italy. That might make him cute enough." Wiggling her eyebrows suggestively, Chloe fanned herself with the open book.

Nora snorted when she laughed. "I'm sure he's some old guy if he's friends with Professor Hoffman."

"That's a shame." Chloe frowned. "You really need a guy."

"I do not want a guy," Nora protested, rising from the bed and grabbing at the shirts piled atop her dresser.

"I didn't say *want*. I said *need*. They have the necessary equipment to help you with your v-card problem."

"You say that like having my virginity is an affliction." Nora glowered at her best friend while she threw shirts into the open suitcase at the end of the bed.

Chloe shrugged. "Maybe a hot Italian guy can convince you to give it up." When her gaze met Nora's she rolled her eyes. "Of course, that won't happen. Not if I'm not there to be your wingwoman. Girl, you *have* to loosen up and have fun while you're on this trip." Waving the book, she stood. "In fact, I want to see pictures of you at all these places, and *especially* on the back of some hot Italian guy's motorcycle." Biting her lip, she glanced to the ceiling. "I think I saw that in a movie once."

"I'm sure I'll be working too much to pick up guys," Nora said, stifling a yawn.

Chloe's expression morphed from playful to concerned. "Did you see that doctor today?"

Nora nodded, covering another yawn.

"And she said you could travel?" A furrow formed between Chloe's brows as she eyed Nora suspiciously.

"She didn't say I *couldn't*," Nora hedged with a shrug.

"Did you even ask her?"

"No," Nora admitted reluctantly as she scratched at the tape holding a cotton ball to the little red dot from the needle stick. "This is ridiculous, you know. People go to the doctor when they're sick, not tired. I just need more sleep. I mean, of *course* I'm tired. I'm taking a full course load."

"Nora, you sleep more than I do, and that's saying something. Is that what she said, that you just need more sleep?"

"You worry too much." Nora turned back to the clothes she dug from her drawers and tossed them haphazardly into the suitcase. She'd organize them later when she figured out exactly what she was bringing and how much she could fit.

"What did she say?"

With a sigh, Nora met her best friend's penetrating gaze. "Nothing. She took some blood to run some tests and said she'd get back to me with the results."

"So, she doesn't have any ideas? When do you get the results back?"

"She said it might be mono. There were some other things she wanted to look into, too."

"When do you find out?"

"The lady in the lab said it could take up to two weeks. Can we be done with the interrogation? You're worse than my mom." Nora sighed and turned back to her open dresser drawer.

"*Two weeks*?" Chloe scoffed. "You won't even find out before you leave. What if you have mono? What if it's something worse? You'll be on an entirely different continent."

"Then I'll go to a doctor there. I can't *not* go to the dig because something *might* be wrong. Can we please not talk about this right now?" Nora pleaded with exasperation.

Chloe pursed her lips and tossed the guidebook at Nora. "Fine, no more talk about doctors. What clothes are you bringing?" she demanded as she moved toward Nora's open suitcase between their beds. "Please tell me you aren't bringing those god-awful cargo pants you wear all the time," she pleaded, pawing through the stacks of clothing. "At least bring a cute dress to go to a fancy dinner or something… Wait, what is this, Nora?" Chloe held up a tattered, black Metallica shirt pinched between her thumb and forefinger like it was some vile creature.

"Oh, it's nothing." Nora reached for the shirt, warmth rushing to her cheeks.

Chloe sighed at her. "Well, that's funny, because I seem to remember some sleazy asshole wearing this nasty thing all the time," Chloe challenged, wrinkling her nose at the shirt and looking over at Nora. "Honey, it's time to let that jackass go. As soon as John realized you weren't putting out, he moved on, it's time you do, too," she chided, holding the shirt out of Nora's reach and sitting on the bed again.

Nora nodded, fighting the stinging of oncoming tears that prickled behind her eyes.

"I know you liked him, but he wasn't who you thought he was."

"I know," Nora whispered with a sigh, thinking back to the way he'd morphed from patient and understanding about her desire to go slow with the physical aspects of their relationship, to relentless in his pursuit of sex. Maybe if she hadn't been so scared and just gave it up to him, he would have been different.

"I see that look on your face. Don't you dare think for one second that you did anything wrong. You are amazing and wonderful, and he was not worthy of you," Chloe consoled, her brows pinched together in concern.

"You're right," Nora croaked out around the frog in her throat. "I just wish I could have done things differently."

"I don't think you're hearing me. He. Him. You could have fucked him every day, and he *still* would have been an asshole."

Nora wasn't so sure that was true. He'd practically been prince charming when they'd met and then one day, everything just changed.

"Okay, I can see I'm not getting through to you, so let me refresh your memory with some harsh realities. Nora, he left you in the parking lot at a concert in the middle of nowhere because you wouldn't give him a blowjob. Do you remember that? Because I do—having been the one to drive for *hours* in the pouring rain to pick you up. I spent more time dealing with the fallout from your relationship than I spent with you," Chloe practically screamed at her. "Stop trying to blame this on yourself. Stop trying to make excuses for him."

Hanging her head, Nora bit her lip and attempted to stave off her threatening tears.

Chloe, undeterred by Nora's emotional distress, continued on her tirade, "I'm sorry to be so harsh, but that's what best friends are for, to give you the big fat reality check and the slap upside the head you need. This isn't some unrequited love where you should keep his nasty shirt to remember him," Chloe reprimanded, wrapping her arms around Nora.

"I know, I'm totally pathetic," Nora said with a sniff. "He was just so sweet in the beginning, I always thought I could get that guy back, you know? Do you remember? He used to bring me flowers and even made me a playlist on my iPod once."

"Yeah, to get into your pants! Guys like that are a dime a dozen. Maybe even more like a penny a dozen. And no one even *likes* pennies! They're sleazeballs who think they can pick some flowers and make you a mix tape and then deflower the virgin."

Nora nodded and shrugged in acknowledgment. "Sometimes, I just feel like there won't be anyone else." Sniffling, she tried not to sound as pathetic as she felt, but failed miserably.

"What the hell are you talking about? I'm sorry to burst your bubble, but I am *not* going to attend this pity party. You should know by now you are nothing less than beautiful and awesome. There is a guy out there for you who will see all of that. You just need a change of scenery. Get out of this small town college crap and go on this incredible adventure!" Chloe yelled in Nora's ear as she squeezed her. "But first, I think we need to take you shopping. Get you some of your own fucking t-shirts," she berated, wrinkling her nose in distaste and tossing John's shirt in the trash bin.

Chloe was right, a change of scenery was exactly what Nora needed.

CHAPTER THREE

Nora's lack of sleep on the plane to Italy was beginning to catch up with her. Professor Hoffman moved at an impressive speed-walk through the airport she was having trouble keeping up with, practically running and weaving around other passengers and jostling a few. Tom and Judy were close behind him, but Nora was having some issues with the wheels on her luggage. One of the wheels continually got stuck, finally catching on the edge of a pillar and the offending wheel was wrenched free of its tiny axle.

"Are you kids all right back there?" Professor Hoffman shouted over his shoulder.

"No!" she yelled from behind as she stopped to examine her luggage. The wheel was nowhere to be found, giving her no discernible method to fix it. Crouching beside her luggage, the prickle and sting of warning for her oncoming tears warmed behind her eyes. This trip was not starting out how she had expected it would. Taking deep breaths to ward off the waterworks, she quickly found it was no use. Other people got 'hangry,' but she got what Chloe always called 'exhaustrated'— exhausted and frustrated. And exhaustrated *always* ended in tears.

"Goodness, Nora, are you okay?" Professor Hoffman's kind voice asked from above her.

Nora looked up, aware she was wearing her ugly-crier face, complete with red-rimmed eyes and splotchy cheeks. Shaking her head, silent tears slid down her cheeks when she rose to standing. She took deep, cleansing breaths and closed her eyes, willing the tears to subside and her composure to return.

"It's busted," Tom announced loudly, interrupting the calm Nora had drawn into herself and choking her with his ever-present cloud of cologne.

"So it would seem," Professor Hoffman observed, frowning down at the splintered plastic. "We'll improvise. Here, you can pull my luggage, and I'll carry yours," he decided with a pitying smile.

After luggage was unclipped and rearranged, Judy pulled her into a quick side-hug. "We're almost there," she reassured with a squeeze before they were off toward the exit again.

In a matter of a few minutes, they managed to find their way to the Metropolitan train to take them to the Tiburtina bus station. It was all a flurry of activity until they were finally seated on the bus with nearly four hours to go until they reached their destination.

Breathing a sigh of relief, Nora closed her eyes to calm the shaking in her limbs and ease her heartbeat back down to something less like she'd just sprinted a mile. They couldn't have been on the road for more than a few minutes before Nora was asleep.

Nora awoke with a start when the bus lurched to a stop and people began chattering all around her as they gathered their belongings and prepared to disembark. Rubbing the sleep and confusion from her eyes, she followed the example of the other passengers and gathered her backpack.

Stepping from the bus, she stood with her Professor and classmates beside the other travelers while they waited patiently for stowed bags. Luckily, their group had been one of the last to board the bus, so their luggage was near the front of the compartment and came out first.

Outside the door, a woman stood holding a sign reading 'Hoffman.'

"Ah! Here we are then," Professor Hoffman remarked, speeding toward the woman.

The woman smiled when the Professor shook her hand. "Welcome to Italy, my friends. *Ciao*, I'm Giana, Mr. Micelli's assistant," the woman greeted with heavily-accented English and a broad smile. "Shall we get you to the villa?"

Without waiting for a reply, Giana headed away from the bus. The four Americans followed her to an SUV and wearily loaded the luggage into the back. Professor Hoffman slipped into the front seat while Nora piled into the back with Judy and Tom.

"Are we ready?" Giana surveyed, smiling at them in the rearview mirror.

"Yes!" Judy affirmed excitedly while Nora and Tom nodded their agreement.

"I am sorry we are not spending any time in Siena today. It is a beautiful city. Mr. Micelli has requested I bring you straight to the villa to get you settled. I am sure you all need some time to rest too," Giana observed, looking at them all in turn in the mirror, though Nora could have sworn Giana's eyes lingered on her longer than the others.

"Indeed," Professor Hoffman agreed with a nod. "Not to worry, though, we are close enough that we should be able to come and explore when there is a break in work. Make a day trip of it. How long until we arrive at the villa?"

"It is a thirty minute drive. Dinner will be waiting for you when you arrive," Giana replied with a smile. "Enjoy the view and we will talk more details after you have settled in."

Nora watched as vast farmland flew past them—fields occasionally dotted with the farms' homesteads and outbuildings. As she watched the green patchwork pass by, she realized this place was more like home than she would have imagined. Here, it was a little bit warmer than it was at home at this time of year, but if she didn't look too closely at the style of the buildings they passed—or that the plants varied from the near-arctic hardiness required to grow at home—she could almost imagine they were still in Minnesota. The mere thought of home calmed her jittery nerves, bringing a smile to her face.

Almost too soon, the drive through the countryside was over and they pulled up to the villa. Giana led them into the house where she pointed out the rooms and showed them the five apartments—one for each of them and one for the woman Mr. Micelli hired to cook and keep house for the duration of their stay. Giana pointed out a few of the house's amenities and led them back to the foyer where she bid them all farewell and informed them both she and Mr. Micelli would meet with them in the morning to discuss business. They each chose a room and dropped their luggage before descending on the food laid out on the table for them.

Nora ate with gusto and then bid her companions goodnight, although the sun was still out.

Once inside the solitude of her new home away from home, Nora collapsed on the bed without even undressing and closed her eyes.

***

Nora woke with the sun shining in her eyes and a crick in her neck. She rolled out of bed and stretched, rolling her neck from side to side. Pawing through her suitcase, she found clean clothes and toiletries then made her way to the shared bathroom. Padding across the stone floor, she closed the door as quietly as she could. She cleaned up as quickly as she could to ensure there was enough warm water for the others, though it already began dwindling by the end of her shower. There might be some conflict in sharing a bathroom with three other people.

Nora and Judy ate breakfast then chatted about the villa and exploring the yard until Professor Hoffman joined them. Their conversation turned to the dig and their speculations about what they might find. Tom barely said a word when he finally joined them. Before long, there was a knock at the door, and the housekeeper emerged from out of nowhere to let Mr. Micelli and Giana into the kitchen.

Nora was completely taken aback when she saw their benefactor. He looked nothing like the middle-aged Italian man in a dark suit and expensive loafers she had imagined. Instead, she was met with a man in his late twenties or early thirties, with light brown hair and brown eyes. Dressed casually in cargo pants and a t-shirt, his clothing showcased his muscular physique. Nora looked over at Judy.

She, too, obviously noticed he was gorgeous by the way she was self-consciously finger-combing her tangled hair.

When Tom took him in, he visibly straightened and his mouth turned up into an almost-sneer.

Professor Hoffman seemed to be the only one who didn't have a reaction to him, other than to stand and shake his hand and pull him into a man-hug, complete with the bro slap on the back.

"Professor Hoffman, so glad to see you guys made it here in one piece." Mr. Micelli laughed while he poured himself a cup of coffee. He took a quick sip and then looked around the table, appraising each of them in turn. "So, this is the team. Let's see, Tom, you're easy to pick out. And you must be Nora," he guessed, looking at Judy, "and that would make you Judy," he concluded, turning to Nora.

Judy giggled beside Nora and tucked her hair behind her ears shyly. "You got us backward, Mr. Micelli," she twittered, batting her eyelashes at him.

Nora watched Tom roll his eyes across the table.

"My apologies, *signorina*. I guess I just have to get to know you all better, so I don't mix you up again. And you can call me Dave," Mr. Micelli apologized with a wink.

"Dave," Judy answered with another giggle.

Nora was ready to kick her under the table to knock some sense back in to her.

"Shall we go over the plan?" Professor Hoffman interrupted, a slight note of irritation in his tone.

"Of course, of course." Dave sighed, placing his cup on the table. "The site is less than a mile down the road from here. You can either walk there each morning, or I have provided a golf cart for your use to travel back and forth. I am planning to turn the historic structure into a luxury spa, so I want to make sure we look around the entirety of the building as well as in areas surrounding the garden to ensure anything buried under there is unearthed *before* I begin building. I would hate to have to either stop construction or tear things up later, should there be some reason for officials involved in antiquities to question my due diligence. Now, the initial item in question is still half-buried where we found it. I didn't have anyone with the right tools or knowledge to treat the item as delicately as I believe it ought to be treated. Thus, the reason you all are here."

Professor Hoffman sat up a bit straighter with the compliment.

Dave continued, "Now, I will be visiting the site periodically while the dig is in progress, but I won't be there every day. Giana will be your day-to-day contact out there. If you need something, go to her. If you have something to report, report it to her and she'll get it to me right away. I know this is just an internship for you guys," Dave perceived, his glance sliding across all three students. "But I expect you to put in your best effort and be as efficient as possible. I don't want to drag this out forever. I intend to build by the end of the summer, so this isn't some indefinite vacation. I want the entire area around the structure examined, including the garden. Are we clear?"

Nora saw Dave's charisma give way to a shrewd businessman who expected nothing less than absolute efficiency of his employees, paid or not.

"You will work a five-day workweek, more if you deem it necessary, Professor. That should leave you plenty of time for exploration. Hell, maybe I'll even join you on some of your excursions," Dave offered, glancing over at Judy and then to Nora with a wolfish smile.

Professor Hoffman frowned. "Let's go see this artifact of yours, then," He rose from his chair and led their party from the villa and down the road.

CHAPTER FOUR

"Nora, will you kindly fetch a new shovel from that shed near the garden?" Professor Hoffman requested with a sigh as he tossed the two halves of his broken spade to the ground.

"Uh, sure," Nora replied hesitantly.

They'd been at the estate, digging along the north wall of the antique structure for nearly a week now. They'd extricated the initial artifact within the first two days of work, and now they were just digging in the general area to make sure they didn't miss any other potentially valuable items. The 'artifact' ended up being nothing more than a piece of broken pottery a few decades old, not exactly Roman, then. In all the time they'd been there, they'd avoided the garden on the other side of the building. They all felt the same creepy vibe when near it, and Nora could almost swear she had heard muffled screaming coming from there at times. Just the thought of it now gave her goose bumps.

Overactive imagination, she told herself as she slowly made her way to the south-facing expanse of stone. When the garden came into view, the hairs on the back of her neck prickled and her arms broke out in more goose bumps. An overwhelming sense of dread nearly overtook her and it required considerable effort to force her feet across the threshold of the capacious garden. She could imagine it was probably something amazing to behold in its heyday. A large cork tree stood at the center, its branches twisted and tangled unto itself from neglect of pruning. A small, wooden bistro table laid on its side, half-rotted, the matching chairs – reduced to nothing more than kindling – scattered over the marble flagstones. Nora couldn't bring herself to encroach any further into the space, getting the distinct feeling she was disturbing a hallowed place.

A far-off shout from one of her colleagues on the other side of the building stirred her from her trance. She pressed ahead to the small potting shed set in a lean-to against the main building, despite the deep feeling of foreboding which seemed to seep into her very bones.

Nora dug through the contents of the dusty building and her efforts were rewarded with two shovels. She grabbed them both, deciding if she brought the pair, then her chances of being sent back here again were greatly diminished. When she re-emerged into the sunlight, an agonizing and otherworldly scream broke through the stillness. It sounded human—almost. Nora tried to convince herself it was just the wind through some opening in the wall that would make such a noise. Despite her convincing, an instinctual urge to flee gripped her. Instead of running away, her feet remained rooted in place, her knuckles white from her death-grip on the shovels.

When another eerie, muffled, unmistakably *human* cry sounded, she sprinted toward the exit of the garden, intent on getting the hell out of there, only to find her conscience and curiosity wouldn't allow her to go any further.

What if there was someone trapped somewhere in the garden? Maybe there was an old well or something she hadn't seen and someone had fallen down it. What if someone was hurt? She certainly couldn't leave an injured person to suffer, but maybe it would be better if she got help. Mentally shaking away her cowardice, she continued to reassure herself there was nothing to be afraid of. *Stop being a coward and go help.* Someone needed her, and it might be too late for them if she ran to get her classmates. That and she wanted, no, *needed* to satisfy her curiosity and find out what that noise was. Her curiosity won out in the end and she crept toward the massive tree, thinking that was where she had heard the screams coming from. As she moved closer, the cold feeling of dread she'd felt upon entering the garden sat like a stone in her gut. When she reached the base of the tree, she heard the heart-stopping scream again and realized it was coming from the tree.

No, from *below* the tree, in the earth beneath its roots. Gasping, realization dawned on her that someone was buried there, *alive*! The thought crossed her mind that this could all be some kind of hoax, but she decided she'd rather feel foolish for being gullible enough to fall for such a prank than to leave someone to die if it wasn't someone's sick idea of a joke.

Quickly throwing one of the shovels aside, she began furiously digging with the other. How long could someone survive down there? Each inch further into the soil, she felt the dread leech further into her, gnawing at her bones. Despite the voice in her head attempting to convince her to abandon her rescue mission, she continued toiling. Sweat dripped down her back and her arms trembled with each shovelful of dirt cast aside. This was harder than she'd initially thought.

Pausing, she listened for the eerie cries from below which had been absent since she began digging. Maybe she *had* imagined it? A muffled yell coming from beneath her feet made her jump back. Well, at least she wasn't crazy.

"Tom! Judy!" Nora shouted weakly, attempting to get the attention of her classmates for help. Even with her unrelenting determination, she'd only managed to dig down six inches into the packed soil. Frowning, she stuck the shovel into the dirt again, everything about this was strange.

"Everything okay?" Tom panted as he pulled to an abrupt stop just outside the garden. "We heard you yell."

"You're going to think I'm crazy," Nora hedged. "But I keep hearing someone yelling, like they're buried down there." She pointed, to the disturbed earth at her feet.

Instead of wary, like she thought he would be, Tom appeared almost relieved. "I thought I was the only one who heard it," he admitted, taking a tentative step through the ruined gate.

"Help me?" Nora plead, barely keeping tears at bay when she handed Tom the shovel. Dread and relief warred within her, at least she wasn't crazy, but what would they find in this hole?

Another wail startled Tom just as his shovel pierced the dirt, his wide gaze snapping up to meet Nora's. Wordlessly, the two of them continued to deepen the hole Nora started.

When the hole reached a little more than a couple feet down, Nora's shovel connected with a solid surface. Scraping the spade across the wood, her stomach roiled when the outline of a coffin came into view.

Tom's worried gaze met hers. "I don't know what we'll find in there, it could be a trapped animal. Stay here, and I'll get Professor Hoffman," he ordered as he ran from the garden.

The previously animalistic sounds morphed into definitive cries of help, accompanied by the soft thud of what Nora could only assume was a fist pounding. Hearing the noise from the other side of a piece of wood spurred her into frantic action, she couldn't just stand and wait for Tom and the professor to return, she had to do something. There was a *person* down there.

"Hang on, I'll get you out of there!" she shouted, her voice cracking with emotion at the thought that some monster had buried a live person there.

Finding a split in the wood of the lid, Nora wedged the shovel in it and twisted. The wood was more rotted than she had expected and gave way with surprisingly little effort. Dropping to her hands and knees, Nora tore desperately at the decaying wood until a large piece broke off. Tossing it to the side, she was ready to comfort and reassure the unfortunate soul beneath it.

Any words of reassurance died on her lips when her gaze rested on the sight of a figure more dead than alive lying in the coffin. The person appeared almost as though they'd been mummified, like something out of a museum display, with gray skin, sunken eyes and tufts of hair missing. It reminded her of a scene from the movie *Seven*, one which had always given her nightmares. She shook off the chill running down her spine, wondering if the body was even real.

When she leaned forward to get a better look, the corpse before her opened its eyes.

Such cold, blue eyes.

"Oh my God," she gasped, a small sob escaping her.

Nora let out a scream when the figure lunged at her from the coffin, faster than she imagined someone so emaciated could move. It had an impressive grip on her throat with one hand and the other tangled in her hair. Nora tried to scream again and was met with excruciating pain in her neck accompanied by the agony of tearing flesh and warm liquid spilling from the wound.

Scrabbling for purchase on the caving wood beneath her, she attempted to push away from her attacker. The pressure of her blood being siphoned from her with every swallow the creature took was the only thread keeping her tethered to reality while the pain clouding her mind made it nearly impossible to register what was actually happening to her.

Blood loss left Nora drowsy and it took a few seconds to realize she was on her back now, staring up into the blurry branches from beneath the tree. I must have lost my glasses, she thought absently as blurry shapes moved above her with the breeze. A pitch-black crow sat perched above her in the tree, cawing a mocking warning that was much too late. Or maybe he was waiting to escort her soul to the underworld. That's what crows did, didn't they? Though she thought it was far more likely, he was calling his friends to dinner as he watched her slide farther from life.

Somehow, Nora felt calm as death loomed over her. She had to admit the grim reaper was far more attractive than she'd imagined, with bright blue eyes and golden locks. He really was good looking, to die for, even. She let out a gurgling chuckle through the torn flesh of her throat at her dark humor when she was literally looking death in the eyes. Death bent toward her and she closed her eyes, waiting to experience the sensation of having her soul separated from her body.

Want to read more?

AUTHOR'S NOTE

If you enjoyed reading *Irrevocable*, please consider leaving a review wherever you purchase your books! I'd love to hear what you think of *Irrevocable*.

Please consider signing up for my newsletter through my website at www.TaraVasserAuthor.com to get updates on new releases, excerpts from my works in progress, and offers for FREE books!

TARA LIVES IN THE FROZEN NORTH IN MINNESOTA WITH HER WONDERFUL HUSBAND AND TWO RAMBUNCTIOUS LITTLE DUDES. SHE IS AN ENGINEER DURING THE DAY, A CRAZY MOM IN THE AFTERNOON AND A WRITER AT NIGHT. SHE ENJOYS SPENDING HER TIME PLAYING IN THE DIRT WHEN HER GARDENS AREN'T COVERED IN SNOW AND LISTENING TO A WIDE VARIETY OF MUSIC THAT INSPIRES HER WRITING — SOMETIMES DOING BOTH AT THE SAME TIME.

CONTACT TARA

- EMAIL -
TaraVasser.Author@gmail.com

- FACEBOOK —
www.facebook.com/TaraVasserAuthor

- WEBSITE —
http://www.AuthorTaraVasser.com

- TWITTER -
www.twitter.com/TaraVasser

- GOODREADS -
www.goodreads.com/author/show/153
25170.Tara_Vasser

OTHER BOOKS BY TARA

Paranormal Romance

The Bloodlust Chronicles

Irresistible – Book 1
Irredeemable – Book 2
Irreplaceable – Book 3
Irrecoverable – Book 4
Irrepressible – Book 5
Irreversible – Book 6
Irrevocable – Book 7

Red

Red – Complete Trilogy

Contemporary Romance

Naughty Novella Series

Naughty Librarian
Naughty Professor
Naughty Nanny
Naughty Neighbor
Naughty Mechanic